VERA'S VICTORY

World War II: As part of the war effort, Vera Carter has been instructed to adapt her Cordon Bleu cooking skills to running a British Restaurant in Norfolk. This is not her only worry — the staff she's been given are all untrained, and don't always get along with each other. And Geoffrey Parkington, the man in charge, seems to have very little sense of humour. But Vera soon discovers there is more to Geoffrey Parkington than she first thought . . .

ANNE HOLMAN

VERA'S VICTORY

Complete and Unabridged

LINFORD
Leicester

First published in Great Britain in 2009

First Linford Edition
published 2010

British Library CIP Data

Holman, Anne, *1934* –
    Vera's victory. - - (Linford romance library)
    1. World War, *1939 – 1945*- -Social aspescts- -
England- -Norfolk- -Fiction. 2. Restaurateurs
- -England- -Norfolk- -Fiction. 3. Love stories.
4. Large type books.
I. Title II. Series
823.9′2–dc22

ISBN 978–1–44480–338–9

Published by
F. A. Thorpe (Publishing)
Anstey, Leicestershire

Set by Words & Graphics Ltd.
Anstey, Leicestershire
Printed and bound in Great Britain by
T. J. International Ltd., Padstow, Cornwall

This book is printed on acid-free paper

A Disappointing Time
For Vera

'Twenty-one today. Happy birthday, Vera!' Vera smiled happily at the young airman as she waltzed in his arms until the gramophone music stopped. The romantic spell shattered when he asked, 'Are you going into the Army, the Navy or the Air Force, Vera?'

Reminded they were in 1942 wartime, she stiffened. 'I don't know, Bill. I've been told I'm not going to be called up . . . I'm curious to know why I haven't been conscripted into one of the services.'

'Have you got flat feet?' Bill teased looking down at her pretty dance shoes.

'No, I haven't!' Vera shook her head as she laughed and stamped one foot on his shiny service shoe.

'Ouch!'

Bill pretended she'd hurt him and

hopped about on one foot.

The joyful party around them was ending and everyone was starting to leave to catch buses or trains to return to their camps, and Vera had to bid her guests farewell.

'Bye — look after yourself.'

'Hurry, or we'll miss the train. Toodle oo, Vera, lovely party.'

'Shut the door quickly, or you'll have the air raid warden after you.'

'Take care. See you next leave.'

The room was becoming empty as gas masks were slung over shoulders and caps put on and the chattering uniformed young men and women left the house. They were going away from the Norfolk town of Lynn, where they had grown up with Vera, to travel to wherever they were stationed in England.

Bill remained until last, to kiss Vera goodbye, and to thank her mother for the party food, which he said was scrumptious.

Vera's mother, Mrs Carter, said, 'You'll have to thank Vera for that. She's the wizard with food and can produce tasty dishes — even with our meagre war rations.'

Bill gave Vera a heart-stopping grin and said, 'I wish you'd come and take charge of our camp's canteen. They think they're feeding the pigs and slosh any kind of food at us.'

Vera laughed, but felt tears in her eyes seeing him make for the door because she didn't want Bill to leave.

However, she knew in these hard war times everyone had to make sacrifices. Her friends sounded jolly enough, although they had been called up and were in uniform, and she envied them their companionship and their uniforms. She wished she hadn't been told she couldn't be one of them.

Bill ushered her outside into the street for a tender kiss, then said, 'I hope it won't be long before we see each other again.'

Planes droned overhead. They both recognised the sound of the Spitfires — in any case the air raid siren hadn't sounded so they knew it wasn't a bombing raid. 'Go to the shelter quickly, if a raid starts,' she said with concern in her eyes.

'Don't worry, I will.' He lingered on the pavement seeming not willing to want to go. 'Vera, I wanted to ask you . . . '

Was he going to propose? She prayed he would so that she would know he felt as keen to marry her, as she was to marry him. 'Yes, Bill?' she said expectantly.

He seemed slightly embarrassed. 'You know I'm being sent to Malta.'

'You told me. When?'

'Soon. They need aircraft mechanics and I'm going to instruct some of the local men to be able to keep our kites in the air.'

'It will be nice for you in the sunshine. I wish I could go with you.' She sighed looking along the damp, dreary-looking street. But at the moment Vera was keen to have his promise to marry her — he might meet another girl out in Malta. 'What is it you want to ask me, Bill?'

He took a deep breath in. 'It is about my dog. You see I can't take him with me, and I'm at my wits' end to know what to do with Gip . . . no-one in my family can give him a home — I wondered if you would look after him for me?'

Flabbergasted, Vera swallowed. Bill's question was not the request she wanted to hear. He thought more about his dog, than about her!

But she loved Bill. And she thought of him going abroad, worried about his beloved dog, so should she accept the disappointment and think that he would have to come back to collect his dog one day — and maybe her too?

'Bill, I know nothing about dogs. And I don't know what kind of work I'm going to be assigned to.'

His brow creased. She felt a stab of compassion for him being parted from his dog, and not knowing what to do with the animal. Would he have to have it put down? She could see he was in a hurry to catch his train, so she had to decide.

'Yes, of course, I'll take him,' Vera said. 'And if I'm sent away, I'm sure Mum would be glad of the dog's companionship.'

'Thanks, Vera. You're a brick — I'll have him sent to you as soon as I can — must dash now.'

He gave her another quick kiss then ran off down the pavement, before she could call after him more than, 'Goodbye, my love.'

For a moment she sighed. It had been a lovely party, and she hoped one day, when the war was over, she would marry Bill. She took her handkerchief out of her pocket to pat away the tears that were running down her cheeks. Everyone, she told herself, had plenty to feel sad about in wartime. But everyone made the effort to keep cheerful — and so would she.

★　★　★

'Mum,' she said after she'd got a grip on herself and come back into the house. 'We are to have another member of the family.'

Mum, who was already collecting the beer glasses and taking them to the sink to wash them, said, 'That's wonderful, dear!'

The two women smiled at each other.

Putting a glass into the soapy water and swishing the glass with the washing up mop, Mum asked, 'You mean I'm going to have a future son-in-law?'

Vera caught her breath. How she longed to be able to say, yes. But she had to say, 'No, Mum. Bill didn't ask me to marry him.'

Mrs Carter turned from the sink and put her head on one side giving her daughter a sympathetic smile. 'Maybe he wants to wait awhile, dear. Wartime is so difficult for young people to decide about their future. They are being split up all the time.'

Vera didn't want to discuss the pain she was feeling, so she said brightly,

'Bill wants us to look after his dog while he's abroad.'

'Oh, so it's love me, love my dog, is it?'

Vera grinned as she took a tea towel to dry the gasses her mother had washed and explained. 'He can't take his dog to Malta, where he's been drafted. So he's worried about what will happen to it when he goes.' She gave a little laugh saying, 'and I dare say, so will the poor dog be upset when Bill's no longer there to look after him.'

Mum frowned. 'How can we feed a dog?'

Vera hadn't thought of that, and for a moment she felt at a loss.

'Well,' she said slowly after thinking about it, 'I can always bring some scraps home from the restaurant when I finish work. Some of the pig swill has some meaty bits a dog would love, and I can get some dog biscuits to eke it out.'

Mum seemed busy with washing the glasses, but Vera knew she was probably just as disappointed Bill hadn't proposed — and instead had asked them to take in a refugee dog.

But her mother didn't say she wouldn't have the dog. Since losing her husband — Vera's dad had died several years ago — Mrs Carter was left alone much of the day when Vera went out to work, and maybe she fancied a doggy companion.

Vera dashed around bringing all the mugs and plates left around the sitting room into the kitchen. She was glad of some work to do.

There was no food left — not a crumb. She smiled to think it had been appreciated but knew people in wartime always ate everything. As she helped to wash the dishes and tidy the kitchen she recollected she'd known Bill since she was a child and had been to school with him. They were childhood sweethearts and the thought of him going abroad would make a big hole in her life.

As Vera snuggled down into bed that night with a stone hot water bottle by her feet, she thought of Bill and prayed he would be safe. She was pleased her party went so well and that she now had the key of the door. She had much to be thankful for.

But her chief concern was what on earth was she going to be doing during the coming war years.

I'm not a miner, a dock worker, a farmer, a scientist, a railway worker, nor is my job in the water, gas or electricity industry. I'm not working in a reserved occupation. So why haven't I been called up? What on earth do they want me to do?

I'm just a very ordinary girl.

The only thing Vera considered she did well, at least people said she did, was that she could cook.

But even that skill she had was difficult to show with the frugal food rationing. Only very small amounts of meat, bacon and ham, butter and cheese, were allowed for each person. Fats were mainly margarine, and any she could save that was left over after cooking the meat and bacon.

Milk and eggs were mainly dried and came in packets and were not easy to cook with. Tea had to be eked out, oh indeed, everything had to be carefully used. And everyone was encouraged to grow vegetables if they could. Even London parks had vegetable, instead of flower, beds.

Everyone was fearful about who was going to win the war. And even if the Allies were eventually successful, how long the conflict would last. Many countries were now engaged in the bitter battle.

In the meantime, Vera felt she had a private battle to win. She must be prepared to accept whatever war work she was given.

Surely she would be told what they wanted her to do next week?

Vera's Role Is Unveiled

On Friday morning the alarm bell woke Vera at seven o'clock. She buried her head under the pillow but soon gave up trying to go back to sleep because she could still hear the sharp ring.

Once she'd decided that there was no choice but to get up, she swung her feet out from under the bedclothes and began the chilly process of getting washed and putting on her dressing gown and slippers in the cold house. But moving about warmed her and when she got down to the kitchen to make a pot of tea she felt ready for anything.

Taking her mother up a cup of tea she said what was uppermost in her mind, 'I should hear today about the war work I have to do. I've been waiting long enough.'

Her mother, sitting up in bed with

her curlers dotted around her head, took a sip of tea and said, 'I know it's unsettling. You've been worried about what is going to happen to you — and so have I.'

Vera sat on the side of her mother's bed with a mug of tea in her hands. 'Can you manage — if I'm sent away?'

'Of course I can, dear. I'll miss you dreadfully, of course. It will be lonely not to have you here, but I'm not the only mother to have a son or daughter working away from home.'

Vera considered that if Bill had proposed, she may have married him and moved away from home anyway. 'You'll have Bill's dog, Gip,' she said with a grin.

Mum laughed. 'Oh yes, but Gip won't be able to bring me a cup of tea in the morning!'

They both laughed.

'Well, I'd better get on,' said Vera, rising, and went to have her breakfast and get ready to leave for work.

Arriving on her bicycle at the restaurant, Vera was immediately busy checking the crates of vegetables that had arrived.

'The boss wants you, Chef,' called one of the kitchen staff.

Vera liked the owner of the restaurant and was happy to trot along to his office to see what he wanted.

Knocking on the door, she was surprised to see another man in the office. He was a tall man. And although quite handsome, he appeared hawk-eyed.

Her boss said, 'Vera, this is Mr Parkington. He is an official from the Ministry of Food.'

Shaking hands with the gentleman Vera decided she didn't care for his dour looks. The gentleman looked like a typical hard faced official who would tell her that her kitchen was full of mice droppings, or that she was using too much hot water to wash the dishes. Or he'd come to say that the five shillings limit on the amount the restaurant could charge for a meal had been cut down to four shillings. Yes indeed, Mr Parkington looked glum enough to enjoy telling her about any kind of new wartime restriction.

Even when the boss began to praise her work the visitor merely nodded. 'Vera is an excellent cook. She has been trained in cookery and is qualified as a Cordon Bleu Chef. Without her I fear my restaurant may not survive.'

Vera smiled at her employer. 'Of course it will. The other chefs know how to make the dishes people like.'

Mr Parkington turned to Vera and forced a weak smile. 'I'm pleased to hear you have good references . . . ' His smile vanished as he went on, ' . . . and feel you can be replaced here . . . '

Vera frowned at him. 'That wasn't what I meant! I like working here.'

He ignored her protest and went on, 'Now what we want you for is to give nourishing meals to hundreds of people a day. It will be nothing like cooking for

15

the few who can afford to eat at a posh restaurant like this.'

'Oh,' Vera exclaimed brightly. 'You want me to cook for the British Army?'

Mr Parkington managed another ghost of a smile. 'Not exactly, Miss Carter. We are setting up a British Restaurant in the town and we want you to run it.'

Vera gulped quickly as she rubbed her hands on her striped apron. 'You mean, Mr Parkington, that you are not asking me, but telling me, that I am to run this soup kitchen?'

The official's face actually showed a touch of humour as he rubbed his chin. 'That's about the sum of it.'

Now Vera knew why she hadn't been called up. She was not being told to serve her country — but to feed her countrymen.

Recovering from the astounding news, Vera asked, 'And where will this feeding place be?'

'There is a church hall in Fore Street we are in the process of converting into a canteen. We need you there immediately to help us organise this kitchen.'

Vera swallowed. 'You mean, I have to leave this job straight away and report there daily to serve food to a horde of people for a shilling a meal?'

'No. Not a shilling,' retorted Mr Parkington, 'you are permitted only nine pence per meal, Miss Carter.'

There she had it. Her war service was to be making endless very cheap meals in a dreary church hall.

Mr Parkington rose to his feet, with the help of a stick. He shook hands with Vera's boss, and then turned to Vera. 'Report at the church hall in town tomorrow morning at six o'clock, Miss Carter. And don't be late. You'll have a great deal to do.'

'Did you say six o'clock?' Vera was shocked. That would mean getting up at five to be at the hall by six. She had enough trouble waking at seven as it was.

'Yes, Miss Carter, you're starting your national service. A six o'clock morning parade is not unusual for service personnel.'

'Oh!' she exclaimed hopelessly.

'I'll be there too,' Mr Parkington said putting on his hat.

She almost retorted, 'that will make things worse', but dared not.

Vera looked at the dismayed expression on her boss's face. He obviously couldn't do anything to prevent this official from taking away his staff and neither could she.

'Mr Parkington,' she said challengingly. 'Who is going to be eating at this British Restaurant? Do I have to bring some scissors so that I can stand at the door and collect their food coupons from their ration books?'

The tall man walked towards the door.

'No,' he replied turning and giving her a hard look. 'When you arrive tomorrow morning you will be told what is expected of you. Now I have another appointment. Good day to you both.' He opened the door and began to leave.

'Don't expect Cordon Bleu meals!' Vera called after him, showing her anger at him throwing such an unpleasant job at her.

His head appeared around the door as he glared at her. 'Miss Carter, I do expect you to be efficient and provide edible meals on time. Or you will indeed find yourself cooking for the British Army.'

What an insufferable man Mr Parkington is, thought Vera as he left.

★ ★ ★

Feeling drained and unhappy, Vera cycled home early, having bade goodbye to her friends at the restaurant. Glumly she pedalled along thinking about having to swap her high-class kitchen for a church hall bake house. Exchange her skilled demi chefs for unskilled women she would have to teach how to cook.

All the fine points of good cuisine were going to be abandoned as she peeled thousands of potatoes and carrots and chopped up onions until her eyes were filled with tears . . . as they were doing now as she biked home.

Why me? Why have they chosen me to run their soup kitchen? Any woman who normally had to prepare family meals could do the job. Why didn't they let me join the forces? I would love to be a motor mechanic and be taught to drive.

Unfortunately her mum wasn't as sympathetic as she would have liked. 'Vera, just be thankful, as I am, that you are not going to be uprooted and sent away from home. You will have a nice little safe job in town until the end of the war.'

It was all Vera could do not to walk out of the sitting room and not the door.

But as the evening wore on Vera began to consider her position in a more favourable light. She was being faced by an enormous challenge. Feeding the hungry was just as important and necessary to do well, as providing food for the delicate palates of rich diners. Yes, Vera began to see that she was being selfish. Everyone had to make the best of what work they were told to do. And the work she had been chosen to do was essential war work, just as any other. And all she had studied about nutrition would be helpful in preparing simple, wholesome meals.

She had her own battle to win.

'I'll show that stiff-necked Mr Parkington what's what,' she vowed.

* * *

Her bicycle journey to work was going to be about as long as she'd had when working at her previous job. Only the hours would be different. Serving daily lunches meant there would be no more very late nights cooking high class restaurant dinners — only a much earlier start every morning whilst it was still dark until sunrise.

21

That morning, Vera remembered she'd forgotten to get some new batteries for her front and back bicycle lamps she needed in the dim early morning light. Her front one wasn't working at present. She just hoped she wouldn't be seen by a policeman biking without lights and went into town on a roundabout route to avoid the police station.

The town clock struck six before she arrived at Fore Street.

So she didn't appreciate being met at the church hall door by Mr Parkington who told her severely she should have lights on her bike.

Bristling, she replied, 'I'm well aware of that, sir. And if you had given me a little time before starting this job I would have got new batteries. I'm sure you are aware the shops don't open until nine o'clock, and you said I was to be here at six.'

He seemed to have no reply for that, but he tackled her about another fault. 'You are to bind your hair up,' he said, looking at her hair.

'Mr Parkington. I always wear a cook's cap in the kitchen. Now what else do you disapprove of — or shall we inspect the kitchen?'

He just glared at her. 'I want to introduce you to your assistants first,' he said. 'They all arrived exactly on six o'clock,' he said pointedly looking at his watch.

Vera propped her bike up against the church hall saying, 'I'm glad I won't be cooking boiled eggs for you, Mr Parkington. You would complain if they were two seconds overdone.'

'Eggs are rationed to one a week, Miss Carter. I don't have boiled eggs. Now let's get started. I'm a busy man.'

Vera felt inclined to tell him she would describe him as something worse than, 'a busy man'.

But he opened the sturdy front door for her.

Inside the large hall was a polished wood floor, and a high ceiling lit by huge windows. The place smelt musty as if it had been locked up for some time. And yet there were signs that the hall was being altered and prepared as a canteen. Stacked tables and collapsible chairs filled one end of the hall. It looked as if a long serving table was being constructed. And there were large rolls of linoleum ready to be laid over the floor.

Three women stood waiting, Vera took them to be her new staff. A trio at first glance she would not have employed if she had had anything to do with it.

'Let me introduce you to everyone,' said Mr Parkington. 'This is Mrs Gladys Munchie. She has volunteered to come out of retirement and lend us a hand. She used to work in a tea shop.'

Vera shook hands with the dear old lady and felt sure she was as nice as pie — but not a lot of use in a busy kitchen.

'Now here is Sally Williams, who has just left school and will need you to teach her — '

'Everything,' interrupted the young Miss Williams. 'I know nothing about cooking — and I don't like housework. Mum said I had to come to work here,' she declared as she was busy filing her fingernails — which were much too long for kitchen work, she would have to tell the girl to cut her talons. One look at her nubile figure gave Vera the message where her interests probably lay, and she doubted if Sally's bush of hair would fit under a kitchen cap.

'Anyway, pleased to meet you,' added Sally with a nervous giggle, which made Vera realise she might be a pleasant girl under her cheap make-up.

The next person wore expensive-looking clothes and high heels, as if she'd come from an interview for a job, rather than expecting to slave in the heat of a kitchen.

'Miss Margaret Smallwood,' said Mr Parkington, 'she tells me she already knows you, Miss Carter.'

Indeed, the third person Vera remembered from her schooldays. Margaret was tall, and looked a confident lady, puffing white smoke from her cigarette.

'Hello, Margaret,' Vera greeted her old school acquaintance with a warm smile.

'Vera! What a lovely surprise to see you again.' Margaret seemed as delighted to meet one person she knew — although she was several years older than Vera.

Vera sensed it might be a bit difficult having to give instructions to a young lady who she used to look up to as a school prefect when she was in her first year.

And thinking the first instruction she'd have to give Margaret was to tell her not to smoke in the kitchen.

'How come you've been sent to work here, Margaret? I would have thought you would be an officer . . . or something.'

Margaret looked a little embarrassed, and Vera wished she hadn't probed into her private affairs. She would find out soon enough. So she quickly asked her about where she lived.

The two young women had lots to talk about, but Mr Parkington's deep voice soon interrupted their chatter. 'Miss Carter,' he snapped. 'We have work to do.'

The enjoyment of meeting Margaret cheered Vera, and she followed Mr Parkington into the kitchen area of the hall.

But her mood changed to one of despair as she looked around at the old fashioned kitchen. 'You can't expect me to prepare food in this Victorian relic,' Vera said. 'It's impossible!'

'What is wrong with it?'

'Mr Parkington, are you blind?'

His eyebrow raised at her rudeness, but the fiery look in his eyes did not deter Vera from going on to say exactly what was in her mind.

'This place is dirty. Unhygienic.' Her eyes looked around the large room. 'And it's ill equipped,' she added walking over to the cast iron oven range.

'It happens to be a very good make of

kitchen range, Miss Carter. Old it might be, but I've seen one still in use, and cooks assure me they are excellent.'

She couldn't argue with that. But then, he didn't have to cook on it. So she quipped, 'Did you see it in a museum?'

He gave a sigh. 'You'll get used to it.'

Her voice rose, as she looked at the dirty wooden table and said angrily, 'I wouldn't peel a carrot in a kitchen like this! Let alone let it near that grimy oven.'

He slammed his stick on the kitchen table with a loud crack that made Vera jump. 'Well, Miss Carter, you'll have to. The regulations state you have to prepare three courses at lunchtime: soup, a main meal and a pudding.'

Vera stood feet apart and crossed her arms. 'Am I to be given a magic wand, Mr Parkington, to help me get all this work done?'

He didn't appear to be in the least bothered by her hostility and his lips twitched. 'No, magic wands are not issued by the Ministry of Food. I wish they were! But you've been given some staff to help you to prepare the place and cook. And while I think of it, I've arranged for some bags of potatoes, carrots, onions, swedes and turnips, to be delivered here this afternoon. Meals must be served from Monday. That is a government order. I have notices to put up around town in my car, and the local newspapers will print an advertisement for this British Restaurant to be opened here.'

Vera quaked. He was made of steel that man. She didn't think she would ever be able to overrule him.

She felt like crying. And noticing a room leading from the main kitchen, she walked into a scullery to hide her distress.

She couldn't think of a worse situation to be in. Her pride was dented. Why should she have to abandon her culinary skills and finely equipped kitchen for this . . . this terrible, grimy, old-fashioned kitchen?

And be expected to produce masses of meals without her excellent staff? To start serving meals on Monday — and it was Friday already.

It wasn't fair to humiliate her in this way.

Suddenly she felt a large hand on her shoulder and swung around to see Mr Parkington had followed her. 'Don't be too dismayed,' he said in a kinder voice, 'years ago I attended a Harvest Home banquet here in this very hall. The ladies cooked a splendid meal using the same facilities.'

Vera almost shrieked, 'But, Mr Parkington, that was pre-war. And they had only one meal to get.'

'True. That is why I have chosen you to do this difficult job. You have the necessary knowledge about food, and how it should be prepared.' He lowered his head to almost whisper in her ear, 'And I'm sure you have the courage to do it.'

Vera looked doubtful.

'Besides, you have me to help you.'

She thought she heard a faint chuckle and looking up at his face saw a glimmer of humour.

Was he serious? She couldn't see him in his fine city suit skinning a rabbit or plucking a chicken.

'Yes,' he said. 'I'll do my best to get you some camping cooking equipment from the army stores — when you let me know what you require. Now cheer up.'

With a sigh Vera responded in a contrite voice, 'I'm sorry to have lost my temper, Mr Parkington. You, like me, are probably only passing on the instructions you have been told to give.'

'That is so, Miss Carter. The Ministry of Food is crammed full of well-intentioned advisors — I'm merely the messenger boy.'

Vera giggled. 'You can tell them that I can only do my best, sir. But I'm not at all sure I'll be able to manage.'

'Of course you will. Why do you think I selected you for the job?'

Had he chosen her?

It was a little unnerving to realise she had been under scrutiny, that he already knew a great deal about her and she hadn't even filled in an application form for the job. But then like all young people being called up she had been for a medical for war work, and they had done some kind of assessment of her, she remembered.

Somehow it gave her the creeps to think he had read all about her — and she knew next to nothing about him.

But then, did she want to? With a bit of luck she wouldn't see him again. He would go back to the Ministry of Food and stay there.

Vera Meets Her Colleagues

The trio of helpers looked at Vera expectantly after Mr Parkington left. Vera lifted her hands and shrugged her shoulders in a helpless gesture. 'I don't know where to start.'

'Let's have a cup of tea,' suggested small, round-faced Gladys with a warm smile.

Vera smiled at her ruefully. 'Splendid idea. But where are we going to get the tea things from?'

Gladys's eyes twinkled as she picked up her shopping basket and put it on the table. 'I've brought some tea and milk, thinking I'd need a cuppa before long. But, oh gosh, I've forgotten the sugar.'

'That doesn't matter, I expect most of us are used to not having sugar in our tea nowadays.'

'I want some,' said Sally.

'Well, you can't have any,' snapped Margaret, who looked in her handbag and fished out a box of matches saying, 'I've got some matches to light the gas.'

Sally put out her tongue at Margaret when she wasn't looking.

'All right,' said Vera, fearing those two were going to give her trouble, unless she kept them well occupied and well apart. 'Let's see if the gas boiler works.'

They all trooped into the kitchen and while they were lighting the gas burner, Sally opened a cupboard and shouted she'd found a huge kettle. After it had been washed it was put on to boil.

The walk-in cupboard was full of kitchen equipment and stacks of crockery — all well worn.

Vera breathed a sigh of relief as she recognised some pots and pans that would be useful.

Sitting around the kitchen table they all talked at once, getting to know each other as they sipped their tea.

They were interrupted by a knock on the door and saw a white haired man standing in the doorway with his cap in his hands. 'Good morning, ladies,' he said politely.

'George Watts!' said Gladys. 'What brings you here? Come in, and have a cup of tea. I think I can squeeze one more out of the pot.'

'Thank you, Gladys. I've come to find Miss Carter,' said George, walking into the room and giving everyone an almost toothless smile. 'Where's the lady in charge?'

'I'm Vera Carter. Can I help you?'

'Mr Parkington told me to come up and 'elp you, Miss Carter. But I don't know what 'elp you was wanting.'

Neither did Vera at that moment, but she was not going to turn down an offer of help from anyone — however old he looked. 'I'm sure you'll be a great help to us, Mr Watts,' she said immediately. 'We are about to start preparing this kitchen to produce a thousand meals a day.'

A low whistle came from Mr Watts' lips.

'Whew!' exclaimed Sally. 'I don't fancy washing up for that lot.'

Vera laughed at the young girl's indignation. 'We'll all do our share. You'll get used to it, Sally.'

Sally pouted. 'I just want to get married and have babies,' she grumbled.

Vera could have agreed with her, but she said brightly, 'Sally, you are about to learn one of the most important skills that will please any man — how to cook a good wholesome meal. It will involve some hard work, some unpleasant tasks at times, but think how popular you will be with the boys when you tell them you're a good cook.'

Sally made a face. 'I don't like having dirty things to do.'

Margaret said, 'If you have a baby you'll have nappies to wash, and you'll get tired looking after children, so don't think motherhood is all that easy, my girl.'

Vera clapped her hands. 'Right then girls — and boys, let's get started cleaning up the place. Let's see what we can find in the way of cleaning cloths, scrubbing brushes, mops and buckets. We'll begin by washing everything. George — I may call you George?'

'That's my name, Miss Carter.'

He beamed at her and she said, 'Now George, pop round to Woolworths will you and get some disinfectant, bars of green scrubbing soap — and some matches if you please. Here's a fiver. Please ask for the receipts so that I can give them to Mr Parkington.'

George seemed pleased to have a job to do and trotted off to get all she wanted, while the women discussed what had to be done, and kettles were put on the gas to boil for hot water.

'Now ladies, I must insist on cleanliness. That means we all have to wash our hands before we start handling food . . . '

'I can't see any food,' said Sally, 'and I'd eat some if I could, I'm hungry.'

'Stupid girl!' spat out Margaret.

Vera turned on Margaret saying, 'I'm

sure you know you are not supposed to be smoking in the kitchen?'

That put Margaret in her place and she took the cigarette out of her mouth and crushed it on the cast iron range before popping the stub into her bag.

Vera then turned to Sally. 'If you value your fingernails, they must be short. So say goodbye to those talons now. You'll have to wait until the war is over before you grow them long again.'

Sally protested, 'But Miss, I like to have them like the film stars.'

'You do as you please, Sally. But I'm warning you nails as long as yours will get broken and cracked doing kitchen work. So trim them.'

Sally gave a loving look at her beautifully shaped nails and Vera said kindly, 'I'll give you some dusting and cleaning to do today, then you will be less likely to break them. You can shorten your nails tonight ready for tomorrow's food preparation.'

Resigned to the authority in Vera's

voice she grinned and mumbled, 'Thank you, Miss.'

But Margaret Smallwood looked disapprovingly at the girl and muttered something.

Vera felt awful having to behave like a sergeant major, issuing orders and telling raw recruits the fundamentals — like: get your hair cut, and stand up straight! — when she was only a cook. So, determined to show that she could roll up her sleeves to sweep and clean like everyone else, Vera was the first to wind a headscarf around her head, and to tie her apron strings around her slender waist, saying, 'I'll start by checking the cooking equipment and food storage areas, so that I can see what we will be needing.'

Gladys took a prettily coloured pinny with a ranched frill from her basket and while she put it on, Vera made a mental note to ask for some overalls for the staff.

Gladys said, 'I can empty the cupboards and get rid of the cobwebs, and wash all the dusty pans, cutlery and crocks. Shall

I go and find some clean newspapers to line the shelves, Miss Carter?'

Vera nodded. She felt like kissing the old lady. She seemed to have the right wartime spirit. She called to Gladys as she took a basin of water towards a cupboard, 'If you find anything badly chipped throw it out.'

Gladys shook her head. 'No, don't throw anything away! In the First World War we nearly always found a use for everything that was broken.'

Chastened, Vera blushed, and said, 'You're quite right.'

Sally said she was happy to climb up on a ladder she'd found in the yard, to dust the higher shelves, windows and light fittings. Vera was pleased to see the young girl's enthusiasm, but she had the feeling she would have to keep an eye on the inexperienced girl — especially as she was giggling and might fall off the ladder. She would ask George to hold the ladder for her when he came back.

Margaret began to tackle the work surfaces and tiled floors with gusto. She didn't seem to need any guidance and Vera was thankful for that.

With everyone working, she had time to consider how she would manage to feed so many people, without many of the ingredients she'd been used to using.

By lunchtime they all wished they had made a meal to eat, and sat down for a rest and another cup of tea, giving Vera the chance to explain basic hygiene needed in the kitchen, and how they would prepare masses of simple meals for hungry people.

George managed to persuade the baker to give them a leftover loaf from yesterday, and slicing it they made sandwiches with a potted paste filling. No-one complained about the simple fare — everyone was too hungry after the physical exercise.

Funnily enough, Vera thought, she was quite enjoying herself. That was until she noticed Mr Parkington had come back to check on how they were getting on.

'I see you've made a good start,' he said looking pleased, 'everywhere has been beautifully cleaned — although I see you've a smut on the end of your nose, Miss Carter.'

'Well, now isn't that observant of you?' Vera said rubbing her nose, but feared she'd only spread a worse smudge over her face. 'What else have you come to tell me is wrong?'

'Oh I haven't come to find fault.'

'So why have you come?' she asked suspiciously.

'I've brought you some tinned food. I expect you have now a clean cupboard where I could put it.'

'And I have a receipt for you, sir,' she said getting the bill George had given her from her pocket.

He looked slightly dismayed at the amount, but took his wallet out and gave her the money. 'Next time you need anything please fill out these order forms.' He produced a sheaf of papers and handed her them.

'Everything in triplicate?' she read looking down at the instructions on the forms.

He gave a dry laugh. 'Everything. It's not my — '

'I know. It's not your rule. It's dreamed up by those mandarins in the Ministry of Food.'

'Indeed, it's official policy. I have to put up with it, and so, too, will you, Miss Carter.'

What could she say?

But it didn't take her long to think of something else. 'We will need overalls, you can't expect the girls to get their own clothes dirty.'

'Right,' he said taking out a small wad of paper made from old cut-up envelopes and then a pen so that he could write it down. 'Anything else?'

'Funny you have mentioned it, Mr Parkington, but we'll need some food.'

He chuckled. 'Write down what you want and I'll see what I can do.'

'You'll have to do better than that. If I say I need some bags of oatmeal it will be no good bringing me bags of salt.'

He became serious again. 'There is no need to be sarcastic, Miss Carter. I'll certainly do my best to get you what you want. But we all have to make do nowadays. I advise you to stock up with tins of Spam and pasta in case you need to fall back on your reserve when things go wrong.'

'Things don't go wrong in my kitchen.'

He just raised his dark eyebrows, and said with a faint grin, 'I'm very pleased to hear it.'

But as he walked away she knew she had riled him and regretted her show of temper. How stupidly arrogant of her to say things never went wrong in her kitchen — of course they did!

And she was sure he was well aware that she was being insubordinate. It was a wonder he hadn't dismissed her before she'd even started the job.

Something told her that he was a man who knew all about failures. His stick told her he'd had an accident of sorts.

★   ★   ★

By the end of the working day everyone was tired. But Vera looked around the cleaned kitchen with satisfaction and congratulated the girls for their splendid work. Most of all she was pleased that they had worked so well together — they had started to become the Lynn British Restaurant Team of Dinner Ladies.

She sat down when her helpers had gone home and began to fill in the triplicate forms for ordering the food. Chewing the end of her pencil to think of meals that would cost only nine pence a head. What a headache it was to have to cook with so limited an amount of ingredients.

She was just locking the hall door, when a noise outside drew her to the street door where she saw a tractor parking outside the hall. A mud-covered young man jumped down from his cab and called to her, 'Afore you go, Miss. I 'ave loads of 'taters, onions, turnips and carrots for you.'

The lad jerked his thumb at the sacks piled high on his tractor.

A Worrying Time For Vera

Vera felt tempted to tell the young lad to come back tomorrow. She was very tired, and had no-one to help her lift the heavy loads into the store-room.

But turning she spied Mr Parkington's car come purring up. He got out and walked towards them. 'Miss Carter.' He gave her a curt nod, then turned to the young farmhand, tapping the tractor with his stick and saying, 'Well done, John.'

'You might have told him to come earlier,' Vera sighed in a cross voice after her busy cleaning day. 'I can't lift all that heavy stuff into the kitchen by myself.'

'See if you can find the porter's trolley in the yard, Miss Carter.'

'Wouldn't it be easier if John drove the tractor into the store room?' asked Vera.

The official from the Ministry of Food laughed as he said, 'I wish he could.' Then returning his stick to his car he came back to the tractor saying, 'Come on, lad, let's get this stuff indoors before it rains.'

Looking up at the sky, Vera had to agree that some threatening clouds were about and a spring rainfall could be heavy, so she darted off to see if she could find a trolley.

In the yard was a rusty trolley and by the time Vera had returned, with its wheels squeaking because it needed a little oil, she saw Mr Parkington had started to take the sacks John was handing him down from the tractor trailer.

She was amazed.

He appeared to be able to carry the heavy loads a short way into the hall without difficulty.

Gaping as she puzzled how the gentleman could pretend to be disabled when clearly he wasn't, she wondered what else this official hid. Why was such an able man doing work any retired man could do?

There was definitely a mystery about him.

'Take the smaller bags of onions, will you?' she was told, and they all set to work with much huffing and puffing, moving all the heavy sacks of vegetables into the store room.

It was raining by the time they'd finished, and dark. And because she had no lights on her bike she anticipated a long trudge home in the wet.

But Mr Parkington had another idea. 'As it's pouring with rain, and you can't ride without lights, I suggest you leave your bike here in the yard so no-one can steal it, Miss Carter. If you tell me where you live I'll run you home and fetch you tomorrow morning at five-thirty.'

It was a good offer of a lift, and a sensible one, because Vera would be able to ask him about food supplies while they rode in his car — she might also be able to find out more about him.

His car was full of stuff. At a quick

glance Vera was surprised to see his back seat had on it boxes of various kinds — and a spade.

'I didn't know you had to dig for victory, too,' she said.

'You'd be surprised what I sometimes have to do in the Ministry of Food Advice Division,' he replied as she settled on the passenger seat and he started the car engine.

'I'd love to know what you do, all day, apart from inspecting kitchens and criticising the staff. You're good at that. But there're not many British Restaurants in this area for you to get your teeth into.'

He gave a short laugh. But said nothing as they set off.

'You're not really lame, either, are you, Mr Parkington? I would say you carried those sacks of potatoes in the hall like a trained navvy.'

'And I would say, you are too inquisitive for your own good, Miss Carter. I would have thought you had enough to worry about in your own job

— without worrying about me and mine.'

She was silent for a while. 'Oh, I'm not in the least worried about you — you strike me as being quite able, yes indeed.' She glanced sideways at him, 'if I was concerned at all, it would be that chip you carry on your shoulder.'

'Ah. And you don't, I suppose?'

Vera frowned. He was right. She really shouldn't criticise him for bearing a grudge. She'd been showing him how appalled she'd been, having to abandon her high-class restaurant job for a wartime feeding kitchen.

'I grant you that, Mr Parkington,' she said with honesty, 'I've certainly had my moan. But now I'll grin and bear it.'

'Good girl,' she heard him murmur.

But she still wanted to know more about him. She'd become even more fascinated to learn why a man of his calibre had been assigned to kitchen duties.

He said, after a while, 'My stick, if you're curious about that, is nothing more than a walking cane, a gentleman's accessory. It belonged to my grandfather. An umbrella might be more useful — especially today. Now, shall we get on and discuss your cooking requirements?'

Vera pursed her lips. 'Well sir. Basic cooking requirements include, meat, fats, sugar and flour, and that sort of thing. Is that coming on a tractor too?'

He chuckled. 'Your milk supply will be delivered by the local dairy. The milkman will come by horse and cart every morning, including Sundays. He'll leave you two churns. The local butcher will take your order for meat twice a week, and the delivery boy will bring it on his bike.'

Vera knew the tiny amount of meat available in wartime wouldn't need a van delivery.

'What about groceries? Flour, margarine, cheese, salt?'

'Give me a list of the things you'll need, and I'll see what I can do for you.'

'I'll write one out tonight, Mr Parkington. But sir, haven't you got other things to do than grocery shop for me?'

He hesitated before he spoke. 'Let me worry about that. Now we are coming to a crossroads, which turn do I take?'

'Left,' she said, 'second house on the right.' She dared not ask him more. He had shut up like a clam.

Vera looked at his hands on the driving wheel. They were well shaped. She was sure he was a capable man. But she did wonder again why such a capable man was doing such a mundane job. She longed to ask him more about himself, but as they had arrived at an uneasy peace, she thought it was better for it to stay that way.

She would do more detective work on him another time. She felt excited, to have such an interesting man to investigate.

She just hoped that when he had stocked her larder with all the groceries she needed he would be off and she wouldn't see much more of him in the future.

Now why should she worry about him, when she'd just been faced with one of the most challenging jobs in her life . . . she just didn't know. She'd started the day thinking she didn't like him. Now she wasn't sure he was that bad after all.

'Goodnight, sir,' Vera said when they arrived at her house and she prepared to hop out of the car. 'Thank you for the lift.'

But he was out and opening the car door for her in a flash as he said, 'Goodnight, Miss Carter. Get in the house quickly or you'll get soaked.'

She didn't know whether to stand on the drive and wave him goodbye as he turned the car around, but something caught her eye as she ran towards the front door and she screamed.

There on the drive was a dark heap of something she almost tripped over.

'What's the matter?' Mr Parkington

had stopped the car and wound down the window.

Without a torch — or an umbrella to keep the rain off her face — she couldn't see well. 'I don't know what it is,' called Vera.

She didn't want to find out either. She stood wondering how she could get into the house without stepping on it, when she was aware Mr Parkington had got out of the car and was by her side. Getting dripping wet as she was.

'It's a dog,' he declared, bravely bending over to see what it was.

'A dog?'

'Indeed, a very wet one. Someone has tied it to the trunk of the wisteria over the front door and left it here.'

Vera groaned. 'Oh dear me. It must be Bill's dog. He said he was going to bring it round. But the poor animal has just been left in the rain for hours by the look of it. Why didn't he ring and get my mother to take him in? It's not like Bill to be so thoughtless. Perhaps someone brought the dog here for him.

But why didn't they let Mum know, instead of just tying him up outside? I don't understand it. Poor Gip is soaked and frightened.'

Mr Parkington obviously had a way with animals and soon had the sodden dog untied, and on its four paws, and was getting whimpers and little barks from the wet, shivering creature.

Vera was shivering herself as she took out her Yale key and opened the front door.

Another piercing yell from Vera made Mr Parkington look towards the hall where the light had just been switched on.

'Quick. It's Mum — she's had a fall!'

There, at the bottom of the stairs, lay Mrs Carter.

Vera Discovers More About Geoff

Kneeling by her mum, Vera was relieved to see she was able to sit up, although dazed, slumped against the newel post.

'Vera,' the old lady said, 'I slipped down the stairs when the front doorbell was rung and couldn't get up.' Her face showed she'd been crying. Vera suspected she'd been there for hours, unable to stand.

'Have you hurt yourself?'

'I don't think so. I just need you to help me get up.'

Mr Parkington pushed into the hall saying, 'Let me help you,' and before Vera had time to stand herself, he had Mrs Carter on her feet with his strong arm around her.

'Fetch a chair,' he said to Vera. 'She

needs to rest awhile, then she should go to bed.'

Vera brought a chair from the kitchen and heard her mother and Mr Parkington getting on like a house on fire.

'Oh, thank you,' Mrs Carter said in a flustered voice, 'I think I may have knocked my head and been unconscious for a while.'

Mr Parkington had produced a torch from his pocket and shone it on her forehead where a bump was forming. 'Yes, Mrs Carter, I would say you have.'

'I couldn't find the strength to stand. I kept thinking Vera would be home any minute. But it got darker and I wondered what had happened to her . . . then I heard a dog barking outside for ages. But I couldn't reach the door.' She gave a sob.

'Here, use this, Mrs Carter.' He handed her a clean, folded handkerchief.

Vera returned with a chair and wanted to comfort her mother, but was told to go and put the kettle on. Seeing

Mr Parkington was reassuring her mother and she could do no better she went into the kitchen.

It was while the kettle was coming to the boil that she remembered the dog. She rushed back into the hall saying, 'The dog. Where's Gip? Has he run off?'

Then she saw the animal being rubbed down by Mr Parkington with a towel he told her he kept in the car. Letting go of the dog, it shook itself violently and licked Mr Parkington's face.

'There, Gip's grateful to you for rescuing him. And so am I, sir.'

Her mother was smiling up at the tall gentleman, who to Vera's surprise came over and, bending down, gave her mum a kiss on the cheek saying, 'I'm pleased to have been of some help.'

'Don't I get a kiss too? I have to thank you for giving me a lift home.' Vera grinned before she swung around to the kitchen to make the tea.

'Actually,' he replied coming after

her, 'you can repay me by making me something to eat. Being an excellent cook it shouldn't put you out too much.'

'Aren't you expected home?'

He shook his head. 'I'm in lodgings and usually get my meals out.'

One more tidbit of information she'd gathered about him. She vaguely wondered if he was married, and living away from home.

'Well it just so happens I do have some scrag end of mutton stew to warm up, Mr Parkington. And I might be able to make four helpings.'

'Four?'

'Well, sir, Bill's dog needs feeding too.'

'So he does. I'll see what I can find in my car.'

While he was gone Vera scrubbed some potatoes and put them on to boil, then cut up a cabbage — nice and finely as she did in the posh restaurant, although she didn't know why she was taking so much care just because Mr

Parkington was going to have supper with them. And just to show off she decided to quickly prepare rhubarb crumble, from the rhubarb grown in her garden, which was a great favourite with the restaurant customers. She soon had the pudding dish in the oven.

What a magic cave his car was. Vera was wide-eyed to see him return holding a bag of dog biscuits, and dog dish and bed.

'My goodness,' exclaimed Vera, 'whatever next, Mr Parkington? I do believe you must have Aladdin's lamp in your car and the genie gets you anything you ask for!'

'No, alas, or I would have brought you a bottle of wine.'

'The dog stuff is just as good on this occasion. I presume you have a dog of your own, Mr Parkington?'

He put the dog bed down in front of the range and called the dog to curl up in it, saying, 'Now, my dear, I don't think we need be quite so formal. My name is Geoffrey — Geoff. And I know you are Vera, Miss Carter, so shall we agree to call each other by our first names off duty?'

'Very well, er, Geoff. Mr Parkington is a bit of a mouthful.'

'And Vera is a very pretty name for a very pretty girl. Faithful, steadfast and loyal it means — I can't think of a better name for you.'

She blushed, but busied herself with the cooking saying, 'I think we are almost ready to eat. Would you ask my mother to come in?'

He did more than that. Vera saw him walking in with Mum on his arm.

The meal was enjoyed — and there was enough to go round. Gip relished his bowl of scraps and dog biscuits.

'Now, I think,' said Geoff, 'Gip should come home with me. As you rightly say I have a dog and can look after two dogs just as well as one — for the time being, that is. Mrs Carter needs to take it easy for a few days after her fall, and she won't be able to cope with a dog she is not used to. Dogs need a lot of looking after.'

Vera was clearing the dishes from the table, and said, 'How can you do that? You live in lodgings and are at work all day.'

'I'm staying at a farm down by the coast and there are people there who take care of the animals. Gip will have to be trained to stay around the farmyard, and not chase the chickens and sheep, but he'll have a good life.'

'Well, that sounds splendid for Gip. And we'll be most grateful, won't we, Mum?'

As no reply came from Mrs Carter Vera looked at her quickly and saw she'd nodded off.

'Sorry, Geoff, she's gone to sleep. She's had a horrid experience today and it's tired her out. I'll get her a hot water bottle and put her to bed.'

Geoff helped to take the sleepy old lady up to her bedroom and Vera came up with two hot water bottles, one for near her feet and one which she wrapped her nightie in.

'I'll let the dog out in the garden, shall I?' said Geoff. 'It seems to have stopped raining.'

'Yes, please do.'

Vera helped Mum have a quick wash and tucked her into bed before racing downstairs.

He was incredible. He had begun to wash the dishes!

'You needn't do that!' said Vera almost snatching the pot scourer from his hands. 'It's a woman's job to be at the kitchen sink.'

Geoff laughed as he wiped his hands on the roller towel behind the kitchen door. 'Don't think I mind, Vera, to be let off the washing up. But I think you should remember that in wartime women are expected to do many men's jobs. So why shouldn't men do women's?'

Vera looked amazed. 'I suppose they do,' she said. 'This war is making everything topsy-turvy.'

'It is certainly changing our lives.'

Vera agreed but suddenly felt too

tired to even think about it.

'Well, it's almost nine o'clock. Gip and I must be off. Now don't expect me to call for you until seven o'clock tomorrow morning. You will have your hands full helping your mother, and making sure she will be all right while you are at work.'

'Thank you, Geoff. For all you have done for us.'

She went to the front door to see him off.

'Wait a minute,' he said, as he bundled the dog, basket and dog dish into the car, and he came back with a package.

'This is for you,' he said, thrusting the bag into her hands and giving her a quick kiss on her cheek.

Before she could open it he was in the car and the sound of the motor prevented her from saying any more.

When the car had swept off down the road, Vera went into the kitchen to open the package and found inside two bicycle lamp batteries.

'I really do believe Geoff really has an Aladdin's cave in that car of his,' she said to the creamy moon lighting the night world.

It was a struggle for Vera to get to sleep that night, tired though she was. Many thoughts were rushing through her head. Economical recipes she could make, such as lentil soup, rabbit pie, braised liver, sultana roll and rice pudding.

And menus she could adapt, were tumbling through her head. And sacks of onions, Bill's lovable, mongrel dog, and Mum's fall, to say nothing of the tall Ministry of Food official, who was just an ordinary man — but she wasn't even sure about that.

★   ★   ★

Morning came too soon.

'How are you feeling, Mum,' Vera asked as she shuffled in wearing her slippers with her mother's early morning tea.

'I'm going to be fine thank you. I'll take things easy today. Glad I haven't got to get up and take the dog for a walk.'

Vera sat down on the edge of her mother's bed and sipped her cup of tea. 'Yes, wasn't that kind of Geoff to take Gip?'

'It certainly was. You are lucky to have such an understanding gentleman to work for.'

Vera thought so too, but knew he could also be the stiff-necked Mr Parkington, her mother hadn't seen.

'Actually I don't exactly work for him. He's from the Ministry of Food and just oversees the British Restaurants in the area. He makes sure I get the food to cook. I'm in charge of the kitchen.'

'Funny that a man like him is an inspector of kitchens. I would have thought — '

'Mum, I must dash and get ready to go to work now. In the larder is some soup in a bowl you can heat up, and some bread and cheese for your lunch.

So you needn't go out shopping today. I'll get supper when I get in.'

Scrambling to get everything done before she left home, Vera was annoyed to hear loud car horn blasts outside the house.

'Oh dear, Mr Parkington has returned,' she muttered grabbing her things as quickly as she could, 'and he doesn't like to be kept waiting by the sound of it.'

But outside she gasped. There stood a jeep.

'Come on, Miss,' called the irate driver. 'I haven't all day.'

'Where's Mr Parkington?' said Vera running up and sliding on to the passenger seat and the jeep moved off straightaway.

'Don't ask me,' the driver told her, 'I was just told to pick you up and take you into town. I don't get paid to ask why. I just drive this American jalopy.'

'It's nice though,' said Vera. 'I'd love to be able to scoot around in one of these. Do you get American chewing gum to go with it?'

'You wouldn't like it in the bad weather, I assure you. The blasted thing is as draughty as hell. I've had one cold after another since I started driving this jeep.'

'Yes, I can see it hasn't got much protection on the sides when the wind blows and the rain pelts down.'

'And the kind of places the Colonel Parkington wants to go to makes it right sandy and muddy. I spent my free time cleaning this jeep.'

Vera almost fell out of the speeding vehicle. 'Did you say, Colonel Parkington?'

'That's 'im. I'm his driver.'

'But, he has a Ford car.'

'I wouldn't be surprised what he has or hasn't got. Or where he's off to next. He's a right strange officer that one.'

Vera sat up rigid. 'What did you say he does?'

'I didn't. It's hush, hush.'

'Oh, of course,' said Vera, pretending to understand.

'Here we are, Miss, safe and sound. Wish I was going into that restaurant like you. It'll be warmer than sitting in this draughty jeep all day.'

'You might find the kitchen gets too hot for you!' retorted Vera. 'Anyway, thanks for the lift.'

Vera could see that an enormous plain sign with the words *British Restaurant* on it had been erected outside the church hall. Stark as it was, as it would be inside. But already a few people were gathering around to read a notice, which had been put on the door.

'Fancy that,' said a woman, 'you won't need your ration book. Anyone can come and get a meal for nine pence.'

'That's a blessing. I can't get enough food for my big boys. I'll send them here once a week to fill them up.'

'It will be a treat for us to go to a restaurant. I've never been to one before.'

'Opens on Monday, it says. It don't

look as if it's ready yet to serve a cup of tea.'

She's right, thought Vera, easing by the women to reach the door. There's lots to be done.

Vera hadn't time to think any more about Colonel G. Parkington.

'I Can't Bear That Woman'

Vera staggered as Sally rushed by her, almost knocking her over, when she entered the hall.

'Hey, steady on — '

'I'm not standing for any more!' the red-faced girl shouted.

'Wait!' Vera commanded before Sally disappeared. 'What's the matter, Sally?'

It was touch and go whether the girl would stay, but Vera, sensing Sally was upset, came up and put her arm around the sobbing youngster.

'I'm sure we can sort out what troubles you,' said Vera soothingly, 'I need you. Please don't go.'

'I can't bear that woman!'

'Who?'

'That Margaret Smallwood. She thinks she has the right to boss me around.'

'Oh dear! Yes, I know Margaret was bossy at school. She used to be a prefect and I remember her yelling at us if we didn't have our berets on straight. She's a perfectionist.'

Vera was holding on to Sally's hand to rein her in. 'She's a bully!' Sally kept saying. 'They delivered some boxes of oatmeal and flour and that kind of stuff for us to cook with. But bossy boots wouldn't wait for you to come. She wanted to tell us where everything should go — it's all, *do this, do that* — that's not right!'

'Come on, let's have a cup of tea, Sally.'

'There isn't any milk.'

'Oh dear!' Vera wished she'd bought a packet of dried milk with her. Then she remembered Geoff had told her that the dairy was going to deliver some. 'Wait a minute. Mr Parkington said the milkman was going to deliver some, let's see if he has.'

Sally sniffed into her handkerchief. 'I don't want that woman telling me what to do all the time.'

Vera took a deep breath in. 'You don't have to, my love. I'm in charge not Margaret. I'm sorry I was late this morning. My mum fell downstairs yesterday and couldn't get up until I got in — '

Sally's eyes rounded, 'Oo-er! Is she all right, Miss? Broken anything?'

'Fortunately, she didn't. But it shook her up a bit. Anyway I can't stand here chatting I'd better get on. Now please come and help me . . . '

'OK, if you don't let that horrid woman near me.'

Vera laughed. She said bracingly, 'I'm no longer a schoolgirl and neither are you. Between us we should be able to put her in her place.'

Giving Sally a conspiratorial wink seemed to reassure the girl and they both went into the kitchen.

Chaos seemed the right word to describe the mess that confronted Vera. There was flour all over the kitchen, as if it had been deliberately scattered about. A chair was upturned and her shoes crunched on shards of glass.

There was no doubt in her mind that Sally was the culprit and had gone wild and emptied a bag of flour all over the place in a fit of rage.

Gladys was sitting on another chair rocking herself to and fro and looking scared.

Margaret was standing feet apart, hands on hips, as fierce as a storm trooper.

'My goodness!' exclaimed Vera. 'The cat has certainly got out amongst the pigeons.'

'And why are you so late?' Margaret boomed at Vera.

Vera made the effort to smile at her. And it was difficult to look at the irate woman who had bullied her as a child. But now things were different and Vera knew she had not only to regain authority in the kitchen, but also to build a team of cooks out of the three very different women.

'I said, why are you so late?' repeated

Margaret staring at Vera accusingly as if the mess all over the floor was all her fault.

Vera ignored her and turning to Sally said, 'Nip out in the yard and see if there's a churn of milk there, will you?'

Sally was only too glad to slip away.

Vera strode into the centre of the room and said brightly, 'I see they have delivered the flour — and if there's any left, shall we start and see if we can cook something this morning? That is, when we've cleared up this mess.'

Her breezy manner took the wind out of Margaret's sails.

'Gladys, I see you're not wearing your pretty pinny today.'

Gladys put her hand over her mouth. 'Oh gosh, Miss Carter — I forgot it!'

'Never mind, I see a pile of white caps and overalls have been delivered for us and I think we should all put our uniforms on now, don't you?'

Gladys smiled at Vera. 'I hope there's one small enough for me to wear.'

Vera laughed. 'I don't suppose the

Ministry of Food thinks of any kind of refinements like that. If you drown in yours, Margaret here will find hers a tight fit because she is a big woman.'

'I'm not big!' protested Margaret, charging up to the pile of overalls and grabbing one, she put it on. 'Look it fits perfectly.'

Vera agreed. 'You look fine. Now let's see about tidying up before we have a cuppa. Accidents often happen in a kitchen.'

Sally stood at the scullery door and nodded happily at Vera. 'Milk's come,' she mouthed.

Vera kept the women amused by telling them about the most spectacular spills she remembered from her student days and soon the kitchen was spick and span again.

Like herself and Mr Parkington, there was an uneasy peace between Sally and Margaret. But Vera congratulated herself that she still had three cooks at the end of the day, and between them they had produced and eaten a dish of corned beef fritters with vegetables.

'One of the difficulties we face . . . ' said Vera, determined to keep their minds on their job, and to keep Margaret and Sally apart so that they did not have the opportunity to have a go at each other, ' . . . is the need to keep food hot to serve to people. It's easy at home to cook something and pop it on plates to serve four people. Catering is a special kind of cooking for lots of people. I want you to use your initiative — '

'What's that?' asked Sally.

'If you had paid attention in school you would know,' cut in Margaret.

'I went to an elementary school. Not a posh school. We didn't learn about things like init it . . . and such like.'

Vera lent over and patted Sally's hand. 'It isn't a subject, like algebra, Sally. It means using your common sense, and thinking of ways of overcoming difficulties. I'm sure Mr Parkington wouldn't have selected you for this job unless he felt you could make a few decisions without being told what to do all the time.'

Sally smiled hesitantly. 'Do you really think so, Miss?'

Vera nodded, and went on, 'We all know how difficult it is going to be for us. Every day we will be expected to have wholesome food ready for the townsfolk. Economical recipes we have to use which need all our care and ideas to make them as tasty as possible. And the diners will be the first to grumble if they don't get their nine pence worth.'

Pacified, Sally gave a wide smile. 'I will try and do my best, Miss Carter.'

'I know you will. We all will. Monday lunchtime we'll have many hungry people in the hall out there. The new lino is on the floor, and George has set out the tables and chairs. We have to practise getting ready a soup, a first course, and a pudding, to give people the energy to carry on the fight to win the war. You know what it is like to cook here now — and if things go wrong at times, why we'll all help each other, won't we?'

Much to Vera's relief, they all agreed.

The sound of loud clapping made the women turn to see Mr Parkington standing in the open doorway. 'Well done, ladies,' he said.

Vera was pleased to see him — at first.

Just as Margaret was a thorn in Sally's side, so Mr Parkington soon became a thorn in Vera's.

She was tired after last night, and exhausted needing to tell her helpers exactly how to do everything. Keeping them all happy and hoping they would learn to cope, when she had the sinking feeling they were making too many mistakes and the food would be inedible. She'd become hot in the face — not just from cooking over the hot oven — but also from dashing around having to explain how to do every kitchen task, when she was used to having assistant cooks who already knew the basic kitchen work.

'What did you tell me to do, Miss Carter? I'm afraid I've forgotten what you said I had to do next,' Gladys Munchie wailed every so often.

Dear old Gladys was so forgetful. Vera had to repeat instructions — and keep her temper.

But, as it was the end of a tiring day, Vera had lost it.

'I really don't need you to come here and tell me all that!' she shouted at Mr Parkington when he came into the kitchen after the clearing up was done and the girls had gone home, and began to put up all kinds of posters around the room about hygiene and food facts.

'It's regulations to have them displayed, Miss Carter.'

Vera pointed to one poster with a picture of a sailor with the words: *Night and day sailors bring you food. They cheerfully risk their lives to guard your food. They don't mind danger, but waste gives them the creeps.*

'This is the kitchen for heaven's sake, Mr Parkington. Put it out in the hall where people eat. We haven't time to read notices. Anyway, we have a pig swill bin for any left over food.'

He came up and said, 'It doesn't hurt to be reminded about our suffering servicemen.'

Vera exploded. 'I don't need to be reminded, Mr Parkington! My boy-friend is in Malta. Being bombed daily he wrote to tell me. I need to forget about the danger he is in.'

The thought of Bill, far away and being bombed, made tears come into her eyes and her bottom lip quiver.

'I'm sorry,' he said in a gentle voice.

She looked at his broad back as he left the kitchen, and hearing his footsteps going away she suddenly felt lonely, and ashamed she'd attacked him when he was only doing his job. She didn't know, but suspected, he had a reason to be upset about something too. He obviously had an important, top-secret job to do. He probably had just as many worries as she had. Besides, it didn't matter if he was Mr

Parkington — or Geoff — he was someone she had now begun to like.

You're an idiot, Vera Carter. Geoff was willing to help you — and Mum — last night. He even arranged for you to get a lift to work in his jeep this morning. And all you have done is to have a temper tantrum. I'm no better than Sally — and she has more excuse because she is little more than a child, she told herself.

She should have thanked him for the lamp batteries he'd given her, and asked him how Gip was. Oh indeed, lots of things she could have asked him instead of being so snappy. She rushed to do the last minute clearing up hoping he would still be around when she's finished.

But he'd left by the time she'd locked up.

As she biked home with her bicycle lamps blazing and feeling grateful Geoff had given her some batteries, her mind switched to thinking about cooking a full-scale menu tomorrow. So far they'd only cooked a small meal for themselves just for practice. Now they had to begin cooking for many more people. She must plan menus, prepare food in advance to store if possible, and stretch the small meat allowance as far as it would go.

Mountains of vegetables had to be prepared. Generously the girls had agreed they would come in next day, although it was a Sunday, to kick-start the programme by practising preparing a three-course meal.

Opening Day Arrives

Vera felt worse about her behaviour when she got home and discovered Geoff had called to see how her mother was.

'He's so thoughtful,' said Mum who was sitting comfortably in the sitting room with a tea tray on a table near her. 'He made me feel better, although I ache all over. He even made me a cup of tea while he was here.'

'Yes,' agreed Vera, 'I'm sure he means well.'

Mum bristled. 'What do you mean, he means well? He's a real gentleman. And Geoff is no fool I can tell. He will always be welcome here.'

Vera didn't want to talk about Geoff, she felt too embarrassed to admit she'd been so rude he probably wouldn't want to come.

When she didn't reply, Mum asked,

'Have you had a good day?'

Vera just collapsed into an easy chair and her tears flowed. 'It was awful! That lot have no idea how to cook — I had to show them how to do everything. Two fight like a cat and dog — and the other can't remember her name!'

'I'm sure it's not that bad. You're very tired I expect. Geoff said he is keeping an eye on you and that you were doing very well. He said it's not an easy job he's given you so he does understand you're under pressure.'

'That puts it mildly.'

'I wish I could help you, love.'

Having had her moan, Vera jumped up and said, 'I'll be all right, Mum. The girls are not that bad really. They're learning fast. Now I'll get us something to eat.'

Supper turned out to be hilarious as Vera related all the incidents that had occurred in the kitchen that day — which had annoyed her at the time — yet now they seemed quite funny as hearing about them, they made Mum laugh.

To Vera's surprise the practice full scale meal on Sunday went quite well and the ladies proudly ate the food they'd cooked. They went home after the kitchen was clean and ready for the following morning, when the restaurant would be officially open for the townsfolk to come and buy a meal.

* * *

Monday morning. It's a big day, thought Vera, refreshed after her night's sleep. The many things she had to remember she wrote down on a pad of paper Mum had made for her from scraps of paper, old envelopes torn up and used paper bags.

'That really was a good idea of yours. Thank you, Mum,' said Vera. 'I can give my assistants a list of things they have to do and they won't need to keep asking me what they should do next all day long.'

'Is there anything else I can do for you?'

'Well if you can look through your recipe books and see if there are any that I could use, or adapt for our meagre rations, it would be helpful. And, Mum, please don't fall downstairs again.'

A quick goodbye kiss and Vera was pedalling so fast along the road she didn't notice at first a car draw up alongside her.

'Miss Carter!'

The voice made her wobble on her bike. Looking she could see it was Mr Parkington leaning out of his car window.

'What do you want?' she asked putting on her brakes, which squealed as she slowed down.

He looked a little crestfallen as he said, 'Only to wish you luck today.'

'Thank you. I'll need it.'

'You seem to have everyone under control.'

She huffed, it was not going to be

easy and she wanted to exaggerate her difficulties. 'Geoff — Mr Parkington — yesterday was near chaos. I expect it will be again today. Mrs Munchie forgot to put the sugar in the pudding, and Miss Smallwood practically hit young Sally with a rolling pin — they don't like each other.'

Geoff laughed.

'You can laugh, Mr Parkington. It's no joke when you're in the middle of it.'

He became serious. 'No, it's not fair of me to laugh. You have done a splendid job so far, Vera . . . And, the girls, as you call them, think the world of you. So do I.'

With that he rolled up his car window and the car moved forward.

She watched his car until it went out of sight.

Well, I never!

* * *

By the time the queue outside the restaurant had reached down past the cinema, George came into the steamy kitchen to report he'd counted roughly two hundred people were out there waiting for a meal.

'I just hope they are not going to be two hundred disappointed customers demanding their money back,' muttered Vera.

George said, 'One man had said he was so hungry he could eat a horse. And a woman with two toddlers said she'd been bombed out in London and had moved to Lynn to stay with her sister — and sharing the kitchen with her was murder.'

Vera tasted the rather weak gravy and commented, 'I've tasted worse. OK, George, let 'em in.

'Margaret will you be in charge in the hall, please? Make sure they've all paid their money to George, and don't charge at the food.'

For the first time, Vera was so glad to have a natural policeman amongst her staff. No-one could organise a crowd of hungry people like Margaret could. She soon had them quiet and in an orderly line while George took their money and Sally began thumping potatoes on the plates, and Gladys gave them a generous helping of cabbage and carrots. Vera took charge of the meat and gravy, careful to portion out the allowance fairly, although some grumbled.

'Is that all I get?' said one big workman looking down at his small ration of brisket of beef.

'That's it,' replied Vera. 'Unless you bring us in another bull to cook.'

'It ain't right to expect us to do a heavy day's work on that.'

'Actually, I agree. But blame Hitler, not me.'

The man grinned. 'I will, Miss, next time I see him.'

Soon the hall was so full some were waiting while others sat and ate.

'Pick up your dishes and bring them over here,' Margaret's booming voice rang out, 'anything that's left on your plate should be put in this bin.'

But there wasn't anything much left.

There wasn't a child who whined about not liking cabbage, or an old lady who said the meat was too tough for her false teeth. Every one seemed to eat everything they were given — with relish.

Vera sighed with relief. She felt pleased. It was always nice when a cook's efforts were appreciated. And even more it seemed to Vera when they were not diners who could afford luxury meals, but ordinary hungry folk thankful for a wholesome plate of food.

Amongst the last few people in line waiting to be served Vera spotted the tall figure of Mr Parkington.

She knew why he'd come, there was no better way of checking on the food being served than having some yourself.

But her hand was trembling as he came nearer and nearer. She just prayed he wouldn't criticise her — or the food — in front of everyone in the restaurant. But he came up like everyone else holding his plate out for a serving.

'Don't say anything,' he put up his hand to show he didn't want her to make any comment about him being there.

So she didn't. She just gave him his portion of meat and gravy — although she was tempted to give him more than his share. She felt sure some dinner ladies would spoil the good-looking man and give him a little extra.

'Thank you, Vera,' he said as she served him. And then he went off to eat it like everyone else.

'Whew, thank goodness that's over,' Vera said staggering into the kitchen with the scant remains of the food.

'They seemed to gobble it up,' said Sally, 'even my potatoes,' she grinned proudly.

'They didn't have much choice,' remarked Margaret as she carried some dishes to the sink to be washed.

While she turned on the tap, Sally put her tongue out at her.

Vera pretended she didn't see because she thought Margaret wasn't being fair on the young girl who'd done very well for her first attempt at cooking and serving a meal. 'You've done well today, Sally. I'll teach you how to make pastry tomorrow and that will make you a proper cook. Very popular with the boys.'

Margaret sniped, 'From what she says she's popular enough with the boys as it is.'

Vera lost her temper and stormed up to Margaret. 'Listen, Miss Smallwood, I have just about had enough of your bullying young Sally. Leave her alone will you. She has a lot to learn, but admits it and is willing to learn. I don't keep getting at you because you don't know how to cook. You're no better than she is.'

Margaret turned around and doused Vera with a jug of water.

Silence reigned in the kitchen as everyone looked at their soaked supervisor.

Shaken, but determined not to allow Margaret to win, Vera said, 'Thanks. That's refreshing. I was too hot anyway.'

She was still shaking the water from her hair when a towel was put into her hands.

'Dry yourself on this,' said Mr Parkington.

He was laughing as he said, 'Well, well, ladies, now I know where the war is taking place.'

Everyone relaxed and smiled at him nervously.

'I came to thank you all for my meal. It was well up to standard — but then I expected it would be with Miss Carter in charge.'

The girls began to clap — even Margaret — and Vera blushed. She said, 'Thank you, Mr Parkington, you are welcome to come again. But please knock before you come into the kitchen, because next time you may find a jug of water is thrown at you.'

Everyone giggled.

He said, 'I'll try and remember that.'

Vera expected him to go on to mention something they'd done that was not quite right. But he surprised her when he went on to say, 'On this special occasion, the opening of the Lynn British Restaurant, I've brought you each a little present.'

He picked up a cardboard box he had brought in with him and opening it he handed each lady a small bunch of spring flowers — baby daffodils and primroses, tied up with pink ribbon, and gave them all a peck on the cheek so that they all blushed and flustered like clucking hens.

'That is most kind of you,' Vera said. She glowed again after his kiss, which she was sure lasted longer than the one he'd given the others, and looked at her pretty little arrangement of flowers.

'I would have preferred some chocolate,' whispered Sally rather loudly.

'Shut up!' hissed Margaret.

'That reminds me, I have some chocolate bars in my car,' said Mr Parkington, smiling at the cheeky young girl. 'If you come with me young lady, I'll give you some.'

Sally was ecstatic when she returned

with five bars of chocolate, one each for the girls, and one for George who said he would give it to his grandson.

After they'd all had a meal and cleaned up, they sat having tea with George and Mr Parkington around the kitchen table enjoying a lively chat about their first experience of cooking for lots of people. Then the girls went home, smiling as they carried their flowers.

'Well done, Vera,' Geoff said, before he left, leaving her with a glow on her face.

Vera looked around the tidy kitchen and sighed feeling surprisingly content — even with her still damp clothes on.

A Trip To London
For Vera

The hard work entailed in producing large numbers of appetising meals everyday was something Vera was used to. But the restrictions imposed by the Ministry of Food made the work monotonous. So to make it more interesting for herself, and the girls, Vera suggested they tried to experiment a bit and come up with varied dishes.

Doubled up with laughter at some of the suggestions that were made, Vera managed to get them thinking of variations and grand titles to give the dishes.

'That's a great idea,' Vera would say, even if she doubted if it would work. But they did discover a few very good recipes that people seemed to like.

Mr Parkington told them he came to their restaurant more than to the others he supervised, because they served the best meals. 'I give the same ingredients to all the British Restaurant cooks, but you lot are the best at cooking it,' he said.

And Vera lapped up the praise, but was keen to tell him that her assistant cooks, were, by and large, becoming dab hands at preparing the plain food.

Nevertheless, she didn't mention the many near disasters. She was still slightly in awe of the hawk-eyed man who could notice details he disapproved of in her kitchen when he popped in to inspect it at times.

They hadn't had a visit from him for some time when he appeared one day — the very day the worst had happened. Margaret was away with a bad cold, Gladys had forgotten to put the potatoes on to boil, and Sally had accidentally dropped the tray of mince slices on the floor — minutes before the restaurant was due to open.

'OK,' said Vera, trying her best to appear calm, 'Put a large container of water on to boil. We'll have macaroni today. Get it out of the store room will you Sally, and measure one and a half ounces per person — '

'I'm no good at arithmetic. How much is that altogether, Miss Carter?'

Oh my goodness! Didn't they teach you anything in school, Sally!

'Get the macaroni,' repeated Vera. 'Gladys, chop some onions will you?'

'How many do you want?'

Vera put her hands on either side of her head just as Mr Parkington arrived.

'Please go away,' said Vera to him. 'We've had a catastrophe. And I must get some macaroni with bacon cooked quickly.'

He took off his jacket, rolled up his sleeves and went to wash his hands saying, 'Right, Miss Carter, what can I do to help?'

Vera had already taken the bacon from the refrigerator and was chopping it into bite size pieces. 'Would you help Sally, sir? She has to put the macaroni in boiling water for ten minutes and stir it every so often.'

He went immediately to assist the young girl while Vera and Gladys started frying the bacon and onions until a delicious smell wafted around the kitchen.

Knowing the urgency of the situation, everyone worked in silence except for the sizzling coming from the large frying pans, and when George came in with a trolley to take the food into the dining-hall, he exclaimed, 'My, what a beautiful smell.'

'Get some parsley from the yard will you, George, and we'll sprinkle a little on the top of each plateful.' Vera was thankful she'd grown some herbs in pots for the kitchen use.

'Are you ready?' she called to her new chef who was explaining to Sally how the macaroni should be cooked until it was 'al dente'.

'Just about,' he replied heaving the large pan over the sieve to strain the cooked macaroni.

'My goodness,' exclaimed Vera, 'you've made enough of it.'

'I'm sure you'll think of a way to use up any leftovers, Miss Carter.'

'I dare say I will,' she smiled at him, relieved that her quick recipe had managed to smooth over the disaster and that not having a menu people couldn't complain that macaroni was not on it.

'I'd like a word with you,' Mr Parkington said to Vera when the meal was over and she was busy clearing up.

Expecting to be told off for allowing her assistants to ruin the original meal, Vera was surprised when he said, 'I want you to go up to London one day next week. There is a lady there who wishes to meet you.'

Crumbs! Vera swallowed. 'What for, sir?'

'To demonstrate your recipes.'

Was it for his wife? Did he want her to cook for a party or something? 'Where exactly do I have to go?'

'To the Ministry of Food.'

The thought of having to spend her day in another kitchen was not exciting.

'Is my journey really necessary?' she asked, quoting the well-known poster: Is your journey really necessary?

'Yep. It is. You will be given a free travel pass.'

Vera looked around her kitchen. She really didn't want to leave it. She'd become attached to the place — and her assistants.

'What if I say no?'

'In wartime it could mean a spell in prison.' He said it in all seriousness, yet Vera suspected he was teasing her, although in fact she was being given no choice but to go.

'Right,' said Vera. 'Tell me the day and I'll arrange to have that day off. And I'll prepare a simple menu with easy things for the girls to make.'

He had already marched her towards the door. 'Thanks for the macaroni meal, it wasn't bad at all.'

'And thank you for lending a hand,' she called after him. Without turning around he lifted his cane in acknowledgment.

How dreary the outskirts of London appeared. Vera was squashed in between two burly soldiers made even bulkier by the kit they were carrying, yet she thought herself lucky to have got a seat at all; the corridors were soon packed with passengers as the train stopped at stations nearer London.

She peered out of the dirty carriage window to see her first glimpse of London since war started.

She remembered, years ago, wearing a pretty dress, going to Wimbledon for the tennis tournament with her mother. Then visiting London seemed exciting. For a treat they would travel first class — and the train was clean. They had a meal in the restaurant car. Now there wasn't even a cup of tea and a sandwich to be had on the long journey — unless you brought your own with you.

'Look at them barrage balloons!' shrieked one boy.

'Bet I can count more than you can,' yelled another.

Indeed the sky was peppered with the huge floating balloons. They were there, Vera knew, to protect against enemy aircraft flying low and bombing London's buildings.

And yet bombs had caused devastation in places. Gaps like giant teeth missing showed where bombs had fallen on a terrace of houses.

'Terrible ain't it?' remarked one soldier.

'That's what we're fighting for, to stop it, ain't it, Miss?' said the soldier next to her giving her a poke in the ribs, and not even removing the stub of a cigarette from his mouth.

Vera didn't say anything.

'A'course, some people don't have to put on uniforms and fight like the rest of us,' the soldier said pointedly.

'Some of us have equally important things to do!' snapped Vera.

'Sorry, Miss,' the soldier said, 'I've been travelling all night and I ain't in the best of moods.'

'That's all right. We all have our troubles,' said Vera. 'My boyfriend is out in Malta and I know how difficult it is for you boys in the armed services.'

A loud screech of brakes as the train slowed and stopped, breathing smoke like a giant dragon.

'Isn't that just lovely?' remarked a sailor seated in the corner of the carriage. 'I expect there's an air raid and we'll be stuck here for hours.'

'Blast. I'll miss my connection,' grumbled a man.

And I'll be late for my appointment. Vera hoped the lady she was going to meet at the Ministry of Food would understand why she was delayed.

But soon the train was shunted and moved forward again.

★　★　★

By the time Vera managed to find a bus to take her to the Ministry of Food she felt like going home. The porter at the

105

desk told her where to find the room she was told to report to.

'Take the lift over there, Miss,' he said pointing to the decorative lift gates.

Vera ignored the contraption as she wasn't sure she'd be able to make it work properly. She didn't fancy being stuck in that ancient lift. So when the porter wasn't looking she nipped up the stairs. She managed to reach the fourth floor, panting, and looked around. Everything was so big, there were so many doors and corridors. She felt like Alice in Wonderland.

'Miss Carter,' said a cheery voice, and turning, Vera saw a small lady with a white overall coming towards her. 'Come along,' she said briskly, leading the way.

Vera followed obediently, glad not to be lost any more.

'Here we are,' she said ushering Vera into a large room where many people sat, dressed in white overalls.

Amazed to find they were staring at her, Vera felt uncomfortable.

'Here's Miss Carter, at last, ladies and gentlemen. Now she can begin the demonstration.'

Shocked to discover they'd been waiting for her, Vera blinked rapidly. 'What demonstration?'

She felt a right ninny when everyone began to laugh.

'This lady cook has been sent to us this morning all the way from Norfolk,' said the lady introducing her to the crowd of students. 'She is not only young, and pretty, as you can see, but is a skilled chef. And Miss Carter has been highly recommended as the best British Restaurant cook in Britain. She has the knack of turning out small food rations into tasty dishes that feed hundreds of our fellow citizens every day.'

Vera had to giggle as she realised she'd been set up by Mr Parkington. But with so many eyes trained on her, there was nothing for it but to start talking about the dishes served up daily.

She smiled at her audience, knowing

at least she knew her subject, and began by saying, 'I wish I was able to wave a magic wand and increase our meat and fat allowance. But I can't, these are austere times, and I have to use vegetables, flour, oatmeal, and pulses to fill up the hungry people that turn up at my restaurant each day.'

'That's just what we want you to tell us about.'

'Oh!' Vera said. He might have warned me to bring some recipes along — I'll just have to hope I can remember some.

The eager faces showed everyone was expecting her to not only tell them about her recipes — but looking at the kitchen equipment, she realised that they wanted her to demonstrate cooking too!

Then she noticed some ingredients were available for her to use.

Her mind whirled.

Um, let me see, I could make a few baked fish cakes with that fresh-salted cod, and make a savoury meat roll, and an almond flan and eggless sponge syrup pudding which is very popular . . .

She was relieved that the ingredient quantities she remembered too.

'Well,' she said, recovering from the surprise, 'my girls and I always start by washing our hands, and having a cup of tea. So, who is going to put the kettle on?'

It turned out to be quite easy for her to show the students how to cook one or two recipes she knew well. She'd stored some basic recipes in her head and she was used to showing her girls how to cook. And having to raise her voice to be heard above the clatter and clamour in a kitchen.

Several members of the audience willingly offered to be her assistants when she asked for help.

Engrossed in her work, Vera found it no problem at all to produce her usual high standards of meals, which were consumed with relish after they were made, and she was inundated with thanks and praise.

It wasn't until she was almost hoarse answering questions, and the room emptied, that she thought of getting back home.

What a day it has been. But I enjoyed it.

Vera wiped her brow as the last goodbyes were said, and she stopped in a corridor to look out of a window covered with criss-cross brown sticky tape to prevent the glass from shattering in an air raid. She could see that the sky was darkening. She gave a shiver. 'Now I have to face a long journey in an unheated train,' she exclaimed out loud.

'Oh, no, you haven't!' sounded a familiar deep voice.

A Trip To London For Vera

It was comforting to see him there. Her boss, her critic — and sometimes friend.

'Geoff!' she said without thinking before she remembered that as they were in the Ministry of Food she should have called him, Mr Parkington. And as the tall man walked easily towards her with a smile on his face, she knew so well, she could only smile back.

'I hear you did very well, Vera. But then, I expected you would.'

Vera's smile faded. 'You tricked me!' she cried crossly. 'You could have told me I was expected to give a talk, and demonstrate cooking some dishes in front of hordes of students. I was scared stiff having to rack my brain to think of some recipes on the spur of the moment!'

His hand cupped his chin as he replied, 'Yes, I should have warned you. But knowing you it would have been an uphill battle to make you come here.'

She couldn't deny that was true.

'So,' he said, 'to make up for my deception I would like to take you out for a nice meal — and of course I'll run you home afterwards.'

Vera's eyes glistened. It was not the meal she was hesitating about. She was sure he had a good one in mind. It was something more serious. She was a single girl alone in London — and he was an attractive man she really knew very little about.

'If you are concerned about your mother, don't be. She won't be expecting you until the early hours.'

Vera gulped. 'I don't know, if I should miss the six-thirty train . . . '

'What you really mean is that you don't know whether to trust me, eh?'

'Exactly. You have a nasty habit of

getting your own way.'

He chuckled. 'I plead guilty to that. Subterfuge is partly my line of business — but not seducing females.'

She looked up into his face and examined it closely. He let her stare at him for a few moments as if he knew she had decided whether she could trust him.

His upright stance and steady gaze seemed to her to be honest. His wide forehead and steely eyes showed him to be intelligent.

And his firm lips meant he could be quite capable of keeping a troop of soldiers under control — but he had kissed her once or twice and she didn't know what she might feel like if he kissed her on the lips . . .

He looked at his watch.

She looked at hers. She had probably missed the early train anyway. 'OK,' she said.

Taking her arm he marched her along the corridor saying, 'The restaurant I have in mind usually serves excellent meals. A small repayment for your work here today.'

'But I'm not dressed — '

'My dear girl, no-one worries about that these days. Anyway, you look perfect to me.'

'I ought to powder my nose.'

'There's a Ladies' Room downstairs.'

While she left him to have a quick wash and brush up, she wondered again if she was making the right decision. He was a powerful man and she was inexperienced. Bill and she were not engaged but had grown up together and their relationship was warm but not passionate . . .

When she rejoined him in the lobby she was not sure that his welcoming smile didn't include a twinkle in his eye that showed he might have some pleasure in her company.

His car outside took them to a smart little restaurant in Soho. They were immediately shown to a corner where there was a table for two. The menu was almost pre-war.

'What would you like to have, Vera?'

'Mmm. Difficult. There's so much that tempts me.'

'Don't hurry then. But don't worry if you hear my stomach grumbling.'

She laughed. 'OK, then, I'll go for the boned duck.'

The waiter seemed to know him. She wondered how many girls he had taken there for a meal. His wife perhaps?

'Do you often come here, Geoff?'

He gave her an amused look. 'Whenever I can.'

'I don't suppose an army officer's pay runs to many meals like this.'

He looked at her straight saying, 'Who told you I was?'

'Your driver of course.'

'Ah. I always suspected that man talked too much.'

'Don't worry, I didn't probe him to find out exactly what you do — apart from grocery shopping for me.'

He laughed. Tossed back the last of his drink and said, 'He wouldn't know my job.'

'So, I'd better not ask you?'

'No.'

She sighed. 'Top secret?'

'Very.'

She sighed. 'Women might have the reputation of being chatterboxes — but some men are just as bad. I wouldn't tell even if you told me.'

'I wouldn't give you the burden of knowing.'

'Is it a burden?'

He called the waiter to pay, saying, 'Believe me it is.'

She studied him again. The lines on his face showed he was not an untried soldier. Something was written on his face she couldn't read. He had suffered she suddenly realised. Maybe earlier in the war? It had given him experience. And that was what appealed to her. Yes, she remembered he'd used a stick when she first knew him. He'd been injured. Suddenly she felt compassion for him. There was so much more she'd like to know about Colonel Geoffrey Parkington.

But she felt he didn't want to tell her, so she said, 'Thank you, Geoff. The meal was wonderful.'

He smiled. 'That's a real compliment coming from an excellent cook like you.'

She blushed at his compliment. 'I just take a bit of care when cooking that's all.'

'I'd call you more than being careful. You're talented.'

'I'm only a cook. Not like you — '

But he would not be drawn into revealing anything about his job and said, 'Now, I'm wondering if you are broadminded, Vera?'

She blinked, twice.

'Don't be alarmed. It's just that The Windmill Theatre is just around the corner and it's a variety show you might enjoy seeing before we go home — that is if you are not worried about its racy reputation.'

She had heard of the famous Windmill Theatre. And the performance's reputation of showing near nudity. Consternation showed on her face.

'I haven't seen the show myself, but they were the only theatre tickets I could get for this evening.'

'Well, I don't know . . . ' The truth was, she felt a little scared all of a sudden being out so late. And she still knew so little about him.

'Come on, we'll go to the foyer and you can see the photographs of the show displayed and see if it takes your fancy.'

They walked along the pavement and were soon outside the theatre. He said encouragingly, 'There are comics too, apart from the showgirls.'

'You have some tickets, haven't you?'

He put his arm around her shoulders and gave her a quick squeeze. 'Of course.'

'So, if I say I'd rather go home, there will be two empty seats in there?'

He looked around to where two sailors were standing looking intently at the large display boards. 'I expect those sailors would snaffle them up if we gave them the chance to see the show.'

Noticing other men, and women, streaming into the theatre, made Vera think the show must be very popular, and it would be a shame to miss the opportunity to see it. Any live entertainment in wartime was a treat — however poor it was.

'OK. I need my provincial outlook widened,' she said, thinking her mum was quite able of looking after herself, even if she came in very late.

Geoff chuckled. 'I don't think you'll see anything in the least educational!'

'It'll be fun for me to go to a London theatre. I haven't been to one before.'

It was exciting to be seated in the cushioned stalls seats, with Geoff by her side.

And as the orchestra struck up and the lights dimmed she was transported into a world of gaiety and laughter. The lively music, colourful stage settings, the jokes — and high kicking dancing girls, made a delightful break as the audience could forget for a spell their daily struggle to cope in wartorn Britain.

* * *

Later, in his car, on the long straight Norfolk road, Vera could hardly keep her eyes open she was so tired.

'It has been a marvellous evening, Geoff. I've enjoyed every bit of it.'

'So have I.'

She yawned.

'Go to sleep,' he said. 'As a soldier I'm used to missing a night's sleep now and again. But you need to be refreshed in order to cope with the mess your assistants have got themselves into by tomorrow morning.'

'Oh, I don't think they can possibly have messed anything up. What I gave them to do was quite straightforward.' She smothered another yawn. 'Although, Gladys might have forgotten something — and Margaret might have upset Sally . . . or vice versa.'

Her voice faded as she had gone to sleep.

She remained fast asleep until they arrived at her house and he shook her gently.

Coming to she murmured, 'Thanks for a wonderful evening. Geoff.'

'I enjoyed it too,' he said giving her a quick kiss on the cheek when he'd helped her out of the car.

He cleared his throat. 'I won't be seeing you for a while. I have to go up to the Lincolnshire coast for some weeks.'

She was half asleep but felt a keen disappointment learning that he wouldn't be around for some time — not even popping in to find some fault in the kitchen which would be better than not seeing him at all.

'Here, give me your key and I'll put it in the lock for you.'

Assisting her inside the house quietly, so not to wake her mother, he left her and she stood in the doorway to wave him goodbye. She found she couldn't move until she could no longer hear his car being driven off.

Her mind was in a dream as she went upstairs and got ready for bed. Partly from the eventful day she'd had, but also because she felt sleepy and confused in her mind. It just didn't seem right to see him go off — knowing it might be days before she would see him again.

Nevertheless, she'd always treasure the memories she'd have of that evening in London she'd enjoyed with him.

A Tragedy For Poor Vera

Waking up next morning, full of the lovely memories of the previous day, Vera was surprised to find her mother had brought her a cup of tea.

Her mother wasn't smiling either, which made Vera sit up in bed and ask, 'What's the matter, Mum?'

Her mother sat down heavily on the end of Vera's bed. 'Drink your tea, dear, while it's hot.'

They sipped their tea and her mum said, 'I've some sad news for you, I'm afraid.'

Vera put her cup down on her bedside table. She had a premonition. 'Bill?'

'Yes, dear. His mother rang me yesterday to say he'd been killed in an air raid on Valetta.'

Vera closed her eyes. Her heart started beating faster. Her Bill had gone forever. She would never see him again. 'Oh, Mum,' she began to weep, 'I loved him so much.'

Her mum was trying not to cry. 'I know you did, dear. And I'm ever so sorry.' She got up abruptly and left the bedroom.

Left alone Vera lay back on her pillows as tears streamed down her face.

She just wanted to die too. Had she been punished for going out and enjoying being with Geoff last night? No, she shouldn't blame herself for having a pleasant evening with another man. Bill had died some days ago, she'd not been unfaithful to him. Although they had not been engaged, Bill would always be locked in her heart. She would miss him terribly.

A knock on her door reminded her that she must get up. 'It's getting late,' called her mother.

Vera knew the hardest thing some people had to face every day in wartime was losing loved ones. And yet they had to get on with their lives. They had to accept that people got killed. Servicemen and women, as well as civilians. Overcoming grief, and being determined to carry on working for victory was expected of those suffering from bereavement. It didn't mean that their loss wasn't hard to bear.

Bill had given his life serving his country. She was proud of him. It took courage to bear the pain of his death. But for him Vera was determined to be courageous and carry on with her war work.

Biking to work with tears that would not stop was dangerous as she was partly blind, and it was just as well she knew the way.

Making sure she had patted her eyes dry, she took a deep breath and entered the kitchen to find the trio standing around aimlessly waiting for her to give them instructions.

'My goodness, girls, what has happened? Has a dog run off with the sausagemeat?'

They didn't laugh.

Vera began to feel worried. 'Tell me what's happened.'

Margaret cleared her throat. 'Vera,' she said, 'your mum rang to tell us your boyfriend, Bill Cryer, has been killed. We're ever so sorry.'

'Yes, we are,' said Sally nodding.

Red-eyed Gladys took out her handkerchief and blew her nose.

That made Vera's good intentions of carrying on as normal collapse as she sat down on the nearest chair. She put her arms on the table and began to sob, not caring any longer to hide that her heart was broken.

Gladys made her a cup of tea — but she hardly noticed it and soon it became cold.

Vera was pleased for once that Margaret was able to take over control of the kitchen.

'Shall we start the stew?' she asked Vera.

'Please do,' sobbed Vera, wishing she could stop crying.

'I'm not taking orders from you!' Vera overheard Sally say a little later, which made her sniff, dry her wet face, and get up on her feet. Crossing over the kitchen to where the two women confronted one another, she said to Margaret, 'How can I help you?'

Sally's mouth dropped open.

Margaret seized the opportunity to say, 'Sally says she won't cut up the vegetables, will you do it, Vera?'

'Certainly, I will,' Vera said going to where Gladys had the vegetables ready to be washed and chopped.

She had just got started when Sally joined her. 'I don't mind doing it with you,' said the naughty girl.

Vera whispered, 'You're not doing this work for Margaret, or for me for that matter. You're doing it for those hungry people outside.'

'Yes, I suppose so. But it makes me so mad the way Margaret orders me about. It's Sally do this, and Sally do that. She doesn't ask me nicely. You should have heard her yelling at me yesterday when you weren't here.'

Vera could imagine it.

'Mum says I shouldn't have to put up with Miss Smallwood's rudeness. She should ask you to do things politely — like you do.'

Vera thought it a pity her mother didn't realise that her daughter was probably exaggerating Margaret's manner of giving instructions. And ignoring the fact that Miss Vera Carter had a sharp tongue when she got in a temper.

She sighed, and said, 'If, in a few years' time, you find yourself in the armed forces, Sally, you won't find the sergeants asking you politely to do anything. I'm told they bark at the recruits, and you'll have to jump to attention and put up with it. So you might as well learn to take orders now.'

Making a face Sally said sullenly, 'I'll wait 'til I have to.'

Vera was slicing the parsnips rapidly in a professional manner. After a minute she stopped and said, 'Margaret isn't that bad. She gets flustered at times when she has a lot to do, just as I do.'

'But you are nice, Miss. She's stuck up.'

'Whether you like it or not, she's more valuable to me in this kitchen than both you and Gladys together.'

Sally chopped violently at a hard parsnip so that bits of it flew off the table on to the floor.

'Hey, steady on, Sally, you'll cut yourself with that knife the way you are attacking those 'nips.'

Too late! Sally yelled as she sliced her hand and blood oozed everywhere.

'Don't stand there dripping blood all over the table, Sally. Go to the sink for heaven's sake, you stupid girl.'

Sally looked contrite and did as she was told without any cheek.

Rushing to the First Aid box, Vera got out some iodine and bandages. First Aid was not her forte, but Vera managed to stop the bleeding, and decided that Sally should go to hospital in case the cut needed to have a stitch or two in it. George was called for to take the chastened girl there.

'I'm sorry, Vera,' Sally said in a humble voice before she was taken away. 'Just when you've had your bad news. I'm ever so sorry.'

Vera could have said the girl should apologise to Margaret, but she didn't. 'Accidents happen in a kitchen, Sally. Just try and be more careful when using the sharp kitchen knives in future. Go home when you've had treatment,' she said, 'there's not much you can do here with a cut hand.'

Now they were very shorthanded.

With her hand bandaged, Sally wouldn't be much use for any job in the kitchen for days, so Vera realised she would have to forget her grief and work harder then ever to help get the meals cooked.

★　★　★

Perhaps it was just as well Vera was busy in the following weeks. Having so much to think about and do with her job she couldn't dwell too much on her sorrow. But it did cross her mind that she missed seeing Geoff, and was surprised he seemed to have disappeared without any contact after their wonderful night out together . . . she'd love to know why.

The days flew by and soon Sally was back at work.

Vera did her best to keep her away from Margaret but the time came when they were close by one another and Vera heard Sally say, 'I saw you pushing a pram when I was off work, Margaret. I'd have thought you'd be out playing golf or something, not looking after babies.'

'Shut up and get on with what you are supposed to be doing,' snapped Margaret.

When Margaret moved away into the scullery, Vera followed her, and was surprised to see Margaret dabbing her handkerchief over her face. 'Are you all right, Margaret?'

As she didn't reply, Vera went up to her and asked, 'What's the matter?'

Margaret turned away. She was obviously very upset. Vera could see her chest rise and fall with emotion.

Taking the crying woman's arm Vera said, 'Come into the yard for a while.'

Vera knew they could talk without being disturbed there. George had managed to acquire an old park bench, which stood on the paved area, so that the girls were able to sit outside for a few minutes in the fresh air. And he tended the small thriving herb garden.

'Sit down, Margaret. Are you feeling unwell?'

Shaking her head, Margaret replied, 'No. I'm quite well, thank you.'

Feeling she wasn't at all happy, Vera said, 'You mustn't let Sally rile you.'

'She's rude. And a gossip.'

Vera sighed. 'I am rude at times too. And most women love to gossip.'

'Well, they should be careful what they say. There's no need to humiliate people.'

Vera frowned. 'So Sally said something she shouldn't have about you?'

Margaret nodded. She buried her face in her hands and cried some more, then blew her nose loudly. 'It's bound to come out now,' she said. 'I can't gag the wretched girl. She will spread it around, I know she will.'

Puzzled, Vera said, 'Well tell me about it. I'll hear all about it sooner or later. Have you robbed a bank or something?'

Margaret lifted her water-filled eyes and as Vera looked concernedly at her she said, 'I have a baby.'

'How lovely!'

'It would be — only I'm not married.'

The words then poured out of Margaret's mouth, 'I used to have a good job in the bank. It was a great life for me before the war. I was stepping out with my brother's friend. We were going to get married after the war, but he got killed.

'Some time later I realised I was in

the family way. Mum and Dad were furious.'

As Margaret screwed up her handkerchief into a tight ball in her fingers, Vera felt sorry for her.

'Then I met Geoff Parkington in town. We were at university together. He was sympathetic when I told him my predicament.' She took in a shuddering breath and expelled the air before she went on, 'Geoff helped me find a flat after Deanna was born, with a lady who was willing to look after her while I'm at work. And he got me this job.'

She patted Margaret on the arm. How hard it must have been for Margaret to have to give up her successful career in the bank and do kitchen work. And do it as well as she did. Smiling Vera said, 'There really isn't a problem for you now, is there? You're well fixed up.'

'If only Sally would shut up.'

Vera pressed her lips together tightly. 'We must think of a way of stopping

Sally from annoying you, then all should be well.'

Margaret's spiky wet eyelashes framed her surprised eyes. 'I wish you could. But I know you have your own bereavement pain — '

'I'll think of some way to shut her up. Now we must get back to work.'

Margaret got up, brushed down her overall, and walked into the kitchen. Vera thought how lucky she was to have a child. How she wished Bill had given her one before he'd died.

Vera collared Sally when she went back into the kitchen.

'Come over here, Sally Williams. I want to talk to you.'

Sally looked at Vera like a mournful puppy. 'I know I was in the wrong, Miss. I shouldn't have said what I said to Margaret.'

Vera didn't ask to know exactly what she'd said. 'Perhaps,' she suggested, 'you could apologise to Margaret for embarrassing her? But if you feel you can't say sorry, then may I ask you to try not to upset her again? She is bossy, I grant you, but she has always been like that since she was a schoolgirl. She isn't getting at you in particular, Sally, she talks to me in a bossy way at times. But she does have a problem.'

'It's her baby, isn't it?'

'Yes. And it's a pity you didn't think of that before you taunted her. Having a baby to look after is a huge responsibility. Especially when the child's father is dead.'

Sally thought about that. Then she asked, 'Is the baby a boy or a girl?'

'She has a little girl called Deanna.'

'Ooh! I love babies. Do you think she'll bring Deanna in for us to see her?'

'I should think she might. You'll have to ask her nicely.'

Sally promised she would.

'Now let's go and get some meals on plates for all those hungry people queuing outside.'

As they returned to the kitchen Sally skipped by her side.

She only wished the pain she felt about Bill's death could be so easily overcome. But people had told her it took time to recover from the loss of someone you love.

Bill will remain in my heart no matter what happens to me.

And having made that vow, Vera was happy to return to the kitchen and give her attention to the meal. Including one small boy who had tripped and splattered his soup all over the floor.

The poor child was shivering with the loud telling-off his mother was giving him. Vera had to hastily give the boy another bowlful, telling the boy, to get it down him quickly, before the Ministry of Food official came in and sent him out of the restaurant for wasting food.

Wide-eyed the boy asked, 'Would he really?'

'I never know what Mr Parkington will do next,' she said truthfully. But she did miss not seeing him — he never seemed to visit them these days.

An Unexpected Meeting

It was a glorious summer morning when Vera decided to take the bus into Hunstanton on her day off.

She wanted to relax by the sea. And recover physically and mentally. To be alone with her thoughts of her lost love, Bill.

The long bus ride was a pleasant change from the kitchen clamour. And she felt excited when she first saw the thin line of blue sea on the horizon and breathed the fresh sea air.

How softly the wind blew her hair as she viewed the sandy expanse of the flat seashore when she got off the bus. She wished it was pre-war days, when she could use one of the beach huts to change into her swimming costume and run over the wide stretch of sand towards the sea and have the little waves creep up over her feet.

Alas, the beach was covered with posts and barbed wire. And *Danger, Keep Off* notices confronted every attempt to get on to the beach.

Even the kiosks that used to sell ice-cream and drinks were boarded up. Memories of what ice-cream tasted like made her mouth water. So Vera decided to walk for miles along the seafront until the houses and hotels were out of sight. Then she found a nice little sandy area in front of an empty round army hideout with slits for rifles to shoot out of, known as a pill box. There she felt cosily private and she could strip off her cardigan, remove her shoes and stockings and push up her dress to above her knees and sunbathe contentedly like a basking seal.

Before long she was disturbed by someone shouting — yelling urgently, crossly.

'Sorry, sir, the dog was so anxious to get down to the beach it slipped its collar.'

Sitting up she put her hand to shade

her eyes and noticed a dog prancing over the sands towards the sea. It was darting in between the posts holding up the barbed wire. And soon the dog was splashing happily in the water.

Putting her hands over her mouth Vera's eyes widened in horror.

Stupid animal! It'll get blown up!

But then the owner was the real stupid one. Fancy allowing your dog to go into so much danger.

She sat stiffly as she watched the endangered animal — yet not wanting to watch it — as she heard the male voice again, bellowing a command, demanding the dog to come to heel.

The dog, having taken a gulp of seawater and being surprised at its saltiness, shook its head and looked towards the shore. Then hearing its owner's voice calling it again it came bounding back over the sand.

Vera closed her eyes and shivered, fearing to hear a loud explosion at any moment.

Alarmed to hear a scampering

around her feet and a lick on her leg, she opened her eyes and saw the dog cocking its head at her for a moment before being called again and off it ran.

It reminded her of Bill's dog, Gip.

Breathing more easily now she realised the dog was away from the dangerous part of the beach, she then sensed she was being watched. Turning her head she blinked rapidly. Standing a little way behind her were a group of uniformed men with an officer — and two dogs.

For a moment she thought one of the uniformed men looked like Geoff. Yes indeed, it was Geoff's tall figure.

'Oh, Mr Parkington . . . ' she began, embarrassed not to know how to address him correctly. And quickly rolling down her dress over her exposed legs.

He didn't look too pleased to see her. 'What are you doing here, Miss Carter?'

'But, why shouldn't I — '

'Get off the beach at once!'

She didn't appreciate being shouted at in that manner. Especially as the last time she had seen him he had been a polite, caring man.

He gave another sharp order to his men. 'Move.' They took themselves off farther along towards some beach huts. One man turned and gave Vera a wink.

As Geoff walked towards her she could tell he was angry. She felt like running away, only she was caught in between the landmined beach and the pillbox.

'You are on army property.'

'Am I? I didn't see a notice.' But then she did see one. Big letters on a notice stated the public were not allowed. 'I must have come the other way and didn't see it.'

'Dogs can't read, but you can, Miss Carter. I could have you arrested.'

Angrily she put her stockings and shoes on and stood up. Without a word she walked away, blindly upset at their unfortunate confrontation. Not even turning back to say how he'd spoilt her day — her much needed rest day.

There were tears in her eyes as the sun on the water made her lower her gaze. She felt miserable. This was not how she had expected to meet Geoff again. As she walked blindly away from him she felt bereft of Bill — and now of Geoff too.

Hearing him calling her she felt she didn't want his company. Then aware he was following behind her she started to run. But he was too fast for her, and a rugby tackle soon had her falling over on the sand.

'Ow!' He'd almost fallen on top of her.

Now she was furious. 'What are you doing?' Being felled by a soldier, where people walking along the promenade might see, was insulting.

'Preventing you from walking into a mined area,' he replied. 'Another step or two and you'd be blown to kingdom come.'

'Oh!'

Another danger crossed her mind as she saw that the two dogs, which he'd had to let go of as he'd raced to save her, were gallivanting joyfully over the sand, enjoying the freedom of a good run.

Being dragged backwards by her ankles was not pleasant. She was hauled to her feet to face Colonel Parkington's wrath.

'How utterly stupid you are, Miss Carter! The beach is mined. Didn't I make that clear to you? Get up that bank immediately.'

'W . . . what about your dogs?' she asked feebly, waving her hands towards the joyful pair of hounds splashing into the water and chasing each other.

'If they die, it will be your fault.'

Covered with sand, as she was, he pointed to steps leading off the beach. Red-faced she climbed them only to find several people gawping and clapping — including a man who gave her a hand up.

She was crying with annoyance, and an old couple comforted her.

'Sit down over here, my dear. There's a cup of coffee left in our flask.'

'Oh no, thank you. You keep it. You'll want another drink before you get home. I'm not hurt at all, just furious with that officer making a fool of me.'

'I think he saved your life. Look, he's managed to get his dogs to come back. I think you all had a narrow escape.'

Vera couldn't deny Geoff had saved her from walking onto the minefield. So it was just ridiculous that for some reason she was unable to feel gratitude.

She felt things had gone very badly between them. First she had strayed onto the beach without noticing the sign to say keep away, and she felt a clot about that. Then seeing Geoff all dressed up in his uniform and telling her off like an incompetent recruit — when she had been longing to see him again. Then being thoughtless and wandering off towards the minefield . . . and risking not only her life but his too.

In less than a quarter of an hour, her

pleasant time at the seaside had become a nightmare.

She couldn't meet Geoff's eyes as he came stamping up to her. He was trying to brush away the sand, which was sticking to his uniform, while the wet dogs shook a spray of water all over him.

Relieved he and the dogs were unharmed, Vera gave a giggle of relief.

'I really thought you had more sense, Vera,' he said angrily. She could see the sweat on his forehead and understood why he was furious with her, as she had been with the dogs. He'd been frightened because all of them could have been injured or killed.

'I, I'm very sorry. I wasn't, I wasn't really thinking, and I don't know what came over me,' she stuttered. She really should have said she was glad no harm had come to him. She couldn't bear to think of him as being injured. But the words would not come into her head. She just looked at him, feeling defeated. Helpless. Tears ran down her cheeks.

His troop of soldiers had come sprinting back when they saw their officer's brave action, and fussed over him.

'Sir, are you all right?'

'I am, thank you. Look after the dogs for me, will you? They'll be tired now and should settle down and sleep until I'm ready to take them home.'

'That was a splendid rugby tackle you made, sir.'

Vera didn't think so as she tried to brush the sand off herself and gain her composure. She could taste the grittiness of the sand in her mouth.

One soldier looked at her, then asked his officer, 'What about the lady? Is she harmed?'

Vera shook her head. Then, fearing she might burst into tears, she walked away with a heavy heart.

Yes, it was awful to contemplate. She had lost Bill — and now she had lost Geoff too.

'Vera!'

A Misunderstanding
For Vera

Hearing her name called, she turned back to see Geoff striding after her. There was no point in running away — he could run faster than she could.

He came up very close. 'The reason I was so alarmed was because I was scared stiff you might be hurt.'

It was just so comforting to have him near and to know that he wasn't as angry with her as she'd feared.

Looking slightly embarrassed he said with a twinkle in his eyes, 'You know, I've told you, I have the greatest regard for you.'

Had he? She didn't remember him saying that exactly. He'd said she was a good cook but that wasn't entirely similar.

The tears running down her cheeks

came back as quickly as she wiped them away. She sniffed. 'I'm sorry, Geoff, it was very silly of me.'

'Let me take you for a cup of tea.'

Vera looked around at the boarded up tearooms. 'I can't see any places here where you can get a cup of tea,' she said.

'I know a place. It isn't far to walk.'

They walked along the seafront in silence. It was strange he was so devoid of conversation, almost as if she had annoyed him so much their relationship had been ruined forever. Had she done the right thing agreeing to go for tea with him when he seemed so unfriendly? Why was he holding back, when in London they had been able to converse freely?

She tried apologising again, but he dismissed her efforts to be contrite.

Something else was bothering him. Was the weight of his two jobs hard for him to bear?

'I suppose you heard about Bill Cryer?' she asked suddenly.

He sounded surprised. 'No,' he said.

'Bill was killed in an air raid in Malta. I was told it happened several weeks ago.'

Geoff stopped walking and grasped her arm. 'Vera, I'm so very sorry. I didn't know that.'

They walked on in silence for a while, then Geoff said, 'How cruel life can be. Losing your fiancé must be so hard for you.'

'Bill wasn't my fiancé. Only I'd hoped to marry him, one day, when this beastly war is over.'

'No wonder you're a little absent minded. I expect you've been thinking about him — missing him.'

'Yes, I have. Today especially when I'm not working, I wish he was here with me.'

They walked a little further and she said, 'The girls at work have been wonderfully kind. They've given me support and got on with their jobs very well.'

He said nothing else until they

reached a hotel. 'Here we are. This is a real old-fashioned place, but they serve good tea and cakes.'

It was a treat to be able to go into a clean ladies room, to wash and brush up. And to sit in plush chairs and have a black dressed, white capped and aproned waitress bring them tea served as it used to be before the war. The tea service was best bone china and very pretty.

The cakes were arranged on a tiered cake stand and it was a pleasure to taste something like the teatime delicacies she used to enjoy.

'So how is your kitchen?' he asked as she poured him a second cup of tea.

She finished her cake, licked her fingers and wiped them on her napkin. 'Fine, I think. We're still serving loads of people every day. In fact more and more seem to come.'

He laughed. 'They know a good place for lunch.'

She smiled. 'It gets a bit weary preparing the same old dishes, but they get eaten. The pigs in the area don't do very well though.'

He laughed again. 'You're supposed to be feeding the population not the pigs, so I wouldn't worry.'

'Talking about animals, how's Gip?' A shadow crossed her face as she thought about what was going to happen to Bill's lovely dog.

He put down his empty cup. 'Well, unless anyone claims him, he thinks he's mine now. Unless your mother wants him?'

'Her leg hasn't been too good after her fall, Geoff. I don't think she would be able to walk him — he's a pretty active dog.'

'That's what I thought. He's used to farm life and he's company for my dog, Battle.'

'Then if you will keep him, I think Bill would be pleased. And I think Gip's a very lucky dog.'

For a while he sat back in his armchair and seemed to be resting. Vera said nothing thinking he had a lot on his mind and needed forty winks.

She hoped he didn't snore because some old ladies had come in for their afternoon tea.

But he wasn't asleep. He opened his eyes and looked at her steadily for some time. She didn't mind because it gave her the chance to look into his eyes, which she considered to be quite beautiful.

'Geoff,' she said suddenly. 'Are we going to win this war?'

'Oh yes. But we have a long way to go. We are in less danger of invasion. We are starting to plan to attack now, after our enemies' first fleeting successes.'

'What do you do? Apart from inspecting British Restaurants.'

He sat up alert and leant forward so that he could talk to her quietly. 'I'm an engineer. I'm involved in the building of a floating harbour. More than that I can't tell you. I have to travel up and down the coast to make sure the parts are being made properly and will fit together.'

'Like inspecting the meals at British Restaurants?'

He gave a wry smile. 'You could say that.'

'Well that should be easy enough for a man like you.'

He turned his eyes away from her and said, 'No. It's not. A lot of lives will depend how well we do this job.'

'Oh, you'll manage it I'm sure.'

Vera was surprised he didn't look comfortable as he shifted in his chair. And she wondered, and asked, 'Surely they wouldn't have picked you to help build the thing unless they knew you could do it.'

'True. I have the qualifications and ideas. But I'm haunted by a past miscalculation — I once made a serious error of judgement . . .'

She had noticed his dour expression ever since she'd first seen him. Now she knew why. He was carrying a heavy burden of regret on his shoulders.

She wanted to suggest he brushed it aside, but he seemed keen to explain his mistake, describing a temporary bridge he'd helped to construct in haste. It had collapsed, and several men had been injured, and one died.

'I'm sure you did your best in a difficult situation, Geoff. An officer's responsibility is not easy to bear. Anyone can look back and see they should have done this, or that.'

She went on to boost his confidence by repeating that he had been chosen and he should forget his past mistake and concentrate on what sounded like an exciting project.

'I can understand why you are worried. It is clearly a big job you've been assigned to do. But you're not the only one working on it I'm sure, and together you will succeed with this enterprise. All you need is to use daring, resolve, to fight our enemies — casting aside any misgivings you may have about your abilities.'

He gave a short laugh. 'You sound like Winston Churchill!'

'Well, I do hear about some things

he says. Like how the war we are fighting involves many nations that have suffered from the evil-doers, and that everyone's war work helps to drive the aggressors from lands they have over-come.'

There, she was lecturing him for a change. But he listened to her advice and then said with sincerity, 'Thank you, Vera. Knowing you have confidence in me is most important for me.'

He looked at her in a way that made her think he did need her. He reminded her of Gip needing a new home.

Funny, she thought, that a strong man like him should be so vulnerable underneath. But then, I suppose we all are.

It was just that he had given her a chance to see not only his strengths but his weakness too.

She looked at her watch. 'I'd better get to the bus station or I'll miss my bus.'

He didn't argue. And she was surprised. Perhaps he was too busy to offer to run her back to Lynn in his car? But she also wondered why he now seemed quite keen to get rid of her.

There was no goodbye kiss from him as she boarded the bus. Perhaps he regretted telling her all he had about himself?

How dreadful she felt seeing him appear smaller and smaller as the bus left the bus station. He waved and then turned away and marched off into the town.

He doesn't want to get too close to me. I'm just his friend.

A sense of loneliness surrounded her as she travelled home.

★   ★   ★

Next day, back at work, she was pleased to see Margaret and young Sally working together amicably. That's one little victory, she thought.

But sweet older Gladys didn't seem too happy as she came up to her. 'Vera, I'm ever so sorry . . .'

Vera raised her eyebrows and waited to hear what Gladys had forgotten to do. And she was amazed to be handed a crumpled letter.

'You see I meant to give it to you weeks ago, but you were busy and I was busy, so I put it in my overall pocket. Then when I got home I saw it and thought I'd better put it somewhere safe. So I put it behind the clock on the mantelpiece where I keep other letters like bills and things . . . '

As Gladys paused for breath, Vera wished she'd get on with it as she was dying to know who had written to her. She didn't recognise the handwriting.

'So when I dusted the mantelshelf yesterday I saw your letter . . . I was appalled to find I had forgotten to give it to you. I suppose I haven't dusted there for ages, I'm so tired after I get home at night, Vera, I just want to sit down with my feet up . . . '

Vera couldn't blame her for that. She often felt the same after work, and she was years younger than Gladys

— maybe Gladys shouldn't be doing a full day's work? Or maybe she should make sure Gladys had a chair to sit on for some jobs she could do.

Gladys was chattering on. 'Anyway, when I saw it I was so upset I'd forgotten to give it to you.'

'Don't worry, Gladys,' Vera said kindly, 'you have a lot on your plate, doing this voluntary work in the kitchen.'

'Oh, thank you. I think sometimes I'm too doddery and forgetful to be as much use here as I'd like to be.'

Vera was tempted to agree with Gladys that she was on occasion more trouble than she was worth in the kitchen. But she was one of her valued trio of assistants and sweet natured to have around — as well as being very helpful at times.

Vera flapped her letter towards the old lady. 'You're a treasure, Gladys. Every little helps to win this war — and you are certainly doing your bit.'

Beaming over her face, Gladys trotted back to where she was working, and Vera was able to open her letter.

She gasped and went out into the yard when a quick glance at the signature told her it was from Geoff Parkington.

It was dated the day after she had been to London.

My dear Vera,

I can't tell you how much I enjoyed your company last night. And I do hope you had just as good a time as I had.

We seem to get on so well, I would like to ask you if I may take you out again — but I know you already have a boyfriend overseas.

However, you may feel it is possible for us to enjoy some time together. Please let me know if you wish to continue seeing me. But if you do not, I will understand and much as I admire you, I will not be a nuisance and pester you.

But I'll always remain your true friend,
Geoff.

Vera put the hand holding her letter on her heart. Every word he had written seemed to convey that he liked her — possibly he loved her. And that it was sincerely meant. It echoed what she felt about him.

But she hadn't replied to his letter . . .

No wonder he'd been so standoffish in Hunstanton. Not hearing from her he'd taken it to mean they were to be no more than working colleagues.

Her mind in turmoil, she didn't know how she got through that day at work. Should she write to him and explain what had happened to her letter? But the words, when she tried to write them once she got home, seemed inadequate.

How do you say you love someone, when they think you have already told them that you do not?

She would have to show him she cared for him. But how could she when he was hopping up and down the east coast visiting engineering works or popping in British Restaurants — including hers

— to see if she was cooking the food properly?

* * *

Later that day, her mother asked her, 'How's Geoff getting on these days?'

Taken aback she replied, 'I haven't seen him for ages. I expect he knows by now that I'm quite capable of cooking hundreds of carrots and potatoes.'

Mum looked at her sharply. 'You'd think he would just call in to say hello, occasionally. But he seems to have forgotten us. Strange, because he seemed a very caring kind of man to me.'

'Oh he is, Mum. Very caring. But remember I told you he has two jobs. I think he feels I'm running the restaurant quite well. So he's concentrating on the engineering work he has to do at present.'

Vera knew that was not the reason for his absence, but wasn't going to explain the real reason why Geoff was avoiding

162

them. She went on to say, 'If Gladys Munchie forgets to put the salt in the spuds it won't matter that much, but if Geoff Parkington is careless, it could be a very serious matter.'

Mum grinned. 'I have the feeling he cares about you too!'

Vera muttered, 'I'd better go and take the flan out of the oven.' She was glad to have the excuse to leave the sitting room and not to have to make a comment about the man who she now knew she loved.

Vera tossed and turned in bed that night. She couldn't sleep for thinking what to do about Geoff. Should she write to him and explain that she hadn't been given his letter until a few hours ago?

But she didn't know where he was. Or, how she should address him — or even which office to send a reply to. It would be too personal, too private for it to be opened by a clerk.

At last she slept, having come to the conclusion that next time she saw him she would explain. When he had written the letter he didn't know her boyfriend had died. And despite the fact she felt she was now willing for Geoff to court her, she felt in no hurry because she had been in love with Bill and needed more time to grieve for him.

In time, she thought, things often sorted themselves out.

Vera Tries To Explain Herself

A few days later she received a phone call early one morning from Margaret who sounded agitated, and in the background Vera could hear a child crying.

'Vera, I'm sorry to say, Mrs Wright, who looks after Deanna, is not at all well, I'll have to stay here and look after her.'

Vera thought quickly. 'Bring her to work with you, Margaret. I'm sure between us we can help you to look after her.'

Vera could tell Margaret was silent as though thinking about the suggestion. 'Very well. I will, if you are sure,' she said with relief in her voice.

'I'm sure we'll manage. Anyway, Sally tells me she loves babies and is dying to see Deanna.'

Margaret sounded surprised. 'She did?'

'Yes, I think our Sally will be only too happy to be looking after Deanna — if she likes babies as much as she says she does, whilst we're busy getting on with the cooking.'

Margaret laughed. 'Right,' she said, 'I'll be along as soon as I can get there. Forgive me if I'm a bit late. I have to get all the baby stuff together.'

'Don't you worry, come when you're ready.'

'Thanks, Vera. You're a brick.'

Vera hoped she wasn't anything like a brick, but she knew what Margaret meant. Wartime meant people had to go out of their way to do things they didn't normally have to do — and today, she suspected, would be chaos.

Shorthanded in the kitchen, with a baby wailing and taking up staff time. And she had a nasty feeling they had run out of packets of dried eggs, and she should have ordered some more, and she hadn't. So she might have to change the menu, and was racking her brains to think of something as she quickly got dressed for work.

'Calm down, Vera,' said her mother.

'It's all right for you,' she said a little tartly as she kissed her mother goodbye, 'you only have knitting to do.'

Mrs Carter was sitting in her armchair, surrounded by balls of khaki coloured wool, and held four small knitting needles, making socks for soldiers.

But she wasn't cross with her daughter as she replied, 'I just hope some soldier appreciates the effort I'm making to make his socks wearable.'

She went back and gave her mother another kiss. 'Sorry, Mum. I didn't mean to say you have an easy time. You're doing your best to help win the war.'

'And I know you didn't mean to be critical, love. I know what's really bothering you — '

Whether Mum did know she was suffering the pangs of being in love, Vera didn't want to find out. She rushed away to clamber on her bike, working up a sweat as she pedalled as fast as she could to work.

But the last thing she expected to see was Mr Parkington's car parked outside the hall.

All the things she'd intended to say to him flew out of her mind. Flustered, she became rosy faced as his tall figure emerged from the car just as she was wheeling her bike through the gates into the yard.

'Hello, Mr Parkington,' she said cheerily, although her heart was thumping with pleasure and anxiety seeing him again. 'I have something to explain to you.'

His face broke into a smile. 'I know. You're out of eggs. I've brought some from the farm for you.'

'Oh! You amaze me. How did you know I needed eggs?'

'They weren't on your order list, and I thought, hey ho, she's forgotten them.'

She wanted just to stand and look at him, to admire his beautiful eyes, but she had to get on.

'Well, I always thought you were a bit of a magician, sir,' she said, 'however, what I have to tell you takes a bit of explaining.'

He walked towards her carrying a large tray of eggs. 'Before you start, Miss Carter, let me put these eggs down first. I don't want to drop the lot.'

As she opened the door so that he could put them on the scullery table he asked, 'Now what is it?'

She wanted to kiss him and say, thank you for the lovely letter.

Saying you like me enough to want my company, and your chivalrous offer to stay away from me because I had a boyfriend already.

She also wanted to explain why she didn't get the letter until recently . . . but it was not the right time to go into all that.

'Margaret Smallwood has to bring her baby into work today. Her baby-sitter is ill.'

'So? I daresay you four women can look after one baby without too much trouble.'

Vera laughed. 'Well, I for one haven't

had much practice. But Sally loves babies and will be a great help. And you can always stay and rock the cradle.'

He scratched his chin as he chuckled.

'I'm better at peeling potatoes,' he said, 'but I can't stay for long.' He was already taking off his jacket and rolling up his sleeves.

'Haven't you more important things to do, sir?'

'Sometimes it helps to have a chance to do a mundane job. It's relaxing for me.'

'I don't find it in the least relaxing,' she said, looking around and seeing everyone waiting for her instructions.

'No, because you are in charge here, Miss Carter. You have the responsibility of making sure the meals are cooked on time. It's the same with me. I have — '

'A heavy responsibility too, I know.'

They looked at each other with understanding.

'Well,' he said, 'I'd better get on with the potatoes. Have you a spare overall I can use?'

Before long the kitchen was buzzing

with workers, and when the baby arrived everyone stopped work to admire the sweet little child. Vera was pleased they soon settled down and the food preparation was on schedule.

'Can I clock off now?' Geoff whispered to Vera. 'I must get back to the office.'

She wanted to say: No, I must have the chance to talk to you. To explain the misunderstanding between them. But it wasn't the time — or the place.

'Any chance of seeing you again — soon?'

She had to think of an excuse for him to come again — quickly.

She went up close to him, as he was putting on his jacket. 'Mr Parkington, there is something else I must discuss with you.'

He looked down at her. 'Couldn't you have mentioned it earlier? I really must go now.'

'No, I couldn't. It's private.'

He looked hurriedly around to make sure no-one was near.

'Right-o, Vera,' he said quietly, 'I'll try to get back to you as soon as I can.'

She watched him go, not wanting to miss a moment of his presence.

'Miss Carter!' shouted Sally, 'Deanna's been sick.'

Vera wasn't surprised, the poor baby had been handed around, kissed and admired, and bounced up and down, ever since she'd arrived.

'Right, Sally. Now, as Margaret is busy, it will be good practice for you, for when you have your own babies, to learn to clean her up. Then take her pram out into the yard, it's a nice day, put her in the shade, and in the quietness out there she should fall asleep after all the excitement she's had. Can you do that?'

'Ooo, yes, Miss, I'd like to do that. It's better than doing them carrots.'

'OK, then. I'll just check Margaret is happy for you to look after her for a while.'

* * *

172

The long day was over at last. It had been successful after all. Everyone had left the hall happy. The diners seemed to enjoy their meal, including the new pudding recipes she'd made for them.

The staff were jolly, and the baby gurgling, when she wasn't feeding or sleeping all day. Sally was convinced she wanted to work with children when the war was over. Nothing had got burned or overcooked and the crockery and knives and forks were all clean and stacked in their trays, ready for the next day.

George had folded the chairs and had stacked them at one end of the hall. He'd swept up after the dinners, and was now washing the lino ready for the dance he held there later that evening.

Vera stopped by to speak to him. 'You do a grand job, George.'

'Thanks, Miss. So do you.'

'I sometimes wonder how you have the strength at your age to do all you do.'

George rested on his mop handle.

'It's difficult at times. When my arthritis plays me up. But I think of all them lads fighting . . . I was in the Great War, you know. In the trenches. It was murder for the lads. So I just carry on, glad to be able to do something to help the war effort.'

'Well, you certainly do that.'

'Lots of people do. Although there's always some that try and take advantage. I have the feeling someone's trying to break in and steal from the kitchen stores. One panel of the yard fence has been loosened so someone can get in. And before long I expect they'll be trying to break the scullery door lock.'

Vera blinked. 'Oh dear. It's just awful to think anyone would do that. You should tell Mr Parkington.'

'I did, Miss, today. He hasn't been here for some time, and I didn't like to worry you. He said he would come as soon as he could and check all windows and doors to make them more secure. I've been patching up the fence damage as best I can. And I reported it to the police and they said they would keep an eye on our yard.'

It spoilt her hectic, but successful, day to hear of this attempted break in. She looked at the old man with sympathy, knowing he had more than enough to do, without the added work this burglary gave him.

And as caretaker he would have to be there this evening while the dance was going on, and prepare the hall in the morning for the people coming for their lunch. Full of admiration for what George was doing for the war effort she asked, 'Can I help you in any way, George?'

'No, no, Miss. You have your hands full I know. And you've got your mum at home to get a meal for now. I'll manage because my friend, Joe, is coming to give me a hand tonight, thank you. Get home now and get some rest.'

It was true she was very tired. She had to bike a long way home and then feed Mum — and she wasn't very good at mending fences — and didn't know anything about door locks for that matter. Hammer, nails and screws were not her usual tools. Although she didn't see why she shouldn't learn to use them. Especially now that women were supposed to do men's jobs.

'OK, George. Let's hope no-one bothers us for the next few nights.'

Although she tried to dismiss the worry from her mind, Vera was very concerned. What if someone broke in and stole their food supplies? What if George confronted them and got injured? It didn't bear thinking about.

The only person she could think of who could help — and in fact it was his job — was Geoff Parkington.

But she knew why he couldn't come immediately to deal with the problem. He had a top-secret job in hand — a tremendous responsibility, a project that may save the lives of hundreds, perhaps thousands of people.

She might have to deal with stopping a break-in herself. After all, women were in the services and were doing all sorts of defence jobs. This was one she should be able to deal with. She didn't want her scarce restaurant food to disappear on the black market, so she would have to act and stop it.

The question was, how?

She would have to get Mum's meal first. Then say she had to go back to help with the dance. Say she'd volunteered to serve tea in the interval or sell lottery tickets to make a little money for those in need, or some such good work so so her mother would approve of her going out at night.

Despite the war, it was surprising that women never felt they were in danger going out at night, even in the dark. There were never any worries about being attacked.

Everyone was well behaved — except for that burglar intent on raiding her store, of course.

She was longing to get her hands on that man. She'd wring his neck.

'I've Been Meaning To Tell You Something'

It was a cold, windy night as it often was in late spring, and even the thought of having to bike into town was bad enough without actually having to do it. But Vera was determined to catch the man trying to burrow into her food store. And it seemed a good night to try and find out who it was because there was a dance going on in the hall. Plenty of people about if she needed help to catch the culprit.

It was a dark ride, and gusts of wind seemed to be determined to knock her off her bicycle, but she pedalled on, at least familiar with the route. Arriving, she put her bike in a nearby shop entrance and locked it.

Although the hall had blackouts she could see slits of light coming from the

178

edges of the hall windows and could hear the dance music coming from inside. It was a local band playing, thumping out the popular tunes. From seeing the cars and bikes outside, and the laughter coming from inside the hall, the dance was being enjoyed by a good-sized crowd.

'Going in to the dance, Miss?' the blackout warden wanted to know.

'No,' said Vera, desperately trying to think of a good reason why she was wandering around outside the building at dead of night. 'I'm going to meet someone.'

'Ah!' He gave a wink. 'Now don't you go doing something you hadn't oughter.'

She laughed. 'There's not much chance of that.'

As they parted and Vera unlocked the yard gate and slipped in to take a look around, she did feel a little peeved to think she couldn't be enjoying the dance instead of waiting for a criminal to appear.

It was cold waiting, too. She huddled

down by the huge pig swill bin and wished she'd thought to wear some extra warm clothes.

A sudden rattling of the yard gate made her start and the strong torchlight searching the yard made her quake.

'Who's there?' a strong male voice called out.

Shuddering, her instinct was to remain hidden.

'Come out, you varmint.'

Vera recognised the big shape of the local bobby, and called back, 'It's only me, Constable Harvey.'

His big feet crunched towards her. 'Well I never, Miss. What, may I ask, are you doing here?'

Vera was glad to stand for a moment and swing her arms around her body to warm herself up. 'I'm waiting for someone, constable.'

'Oh, are you now, Miss Carter? Funny place to wait, next to that smelly bin.'

Vera agreed she might have found a better place but looking around she decided it probably was the best spot to hide in the yard.

'It's only waste food we put out this morning, constable,' she said.

'Well, I suppose you know what you're doing, Miss.'

'Please don't shine that light in my face any more, constable.'

He swung the beam away from her saying, 'I hope who it is you're waiting for won't be long, or you'll freeze to death in this wind.'

'I'll be all right, thank you.'

'Good evening, Miss,' he said, shifting his great cloak over his shoulders as he stamped off shining his light ahead of him.

She was beginning to think she couldn't stand the cold any longer and would have to give up waiting, when she heard another person approaching the yard.

With a gasp of breath, she froze.

Now she felt sure it was the person she'd been waiting for. Someone picking away at a fence panel — they obviously didn't have a key to let themselves into the yard like the caretaker and the constable.

She held her breath. Now she was worried. What if the person was big and strong — would she be attacked?

Too late to think of that! She was stuck. She couldn't hide anywhere else.

For a seemingly long time she heard the fence being attacked and then a creak as the panel gave way, and soon afterwards she could just make out a thin figure coming towards her.

Frightened out of her wits for a moment, Vera almost screamed until she saw the person was only a girl.

Without looking around the girl went quickly over the yard towards the swill bin, opened the lid and began to remove some of the food, which she put in a bowl she was carrying. So intent was she on collecting the thrown away food, she didn't notice Vera there in the dark — at first.

The girl gave a scream and dropped the bowl with a clatter when she became aware of Vera and dashed towards the fence to escape. But an anguished cry told Vera that someone was waiting on the other side of the fence, and the thief had been nabbed.

Vera didn't have to wait long before she was aware that the yard gate had been opened and outside stood the constable, who was holding the girl, and Mr Parkington who looked at Vera in amazement.

'What are you doing here?' he asked.

'I think I have the same reason to be here as you, Mr Parkington,' Vera replied sharply — although she was delighted to see him.

'You really should be at home, you're shivering.' Mr Parkington removed his greatcoat and put it around Vera's shoulders.

It was beautifully warm.

'Now what have we here?' said Constable Harvey shining his torch into the frightened girl's face. 'What's your name?'

Vera could see she was too scared to

speak and said, 'Let's go inside the scullery and discuss this matter sensibly.'

Once inside the girl started to sob. Vera went to get cups of tea from the urn that had been made for the dancers.

'Here, drink this,' she said putting a cup into the girl's thin hands.

Then she turned to the two men. 'Now I suggest you two leave us alone to have a chat. This frightened girl won't explain what she is doing while you two men are breathing down her neck.'

Mr Parkington nudged the policeman and they walked away chatting.

The girl took a few gulps of tea and said, 'I was only getting something to eat, Miss. I didn't think anyone would mind if I had the food that was going to the pigs.'

'Except the pigs,' said Vera with a wry grin. 'Now, what did you say your name was?'

Her narrow face showed she was

deciding whether to trust Vera, but eventually she cast her eyes down and said with a sniff, 'I'm Mary Smith, Miss.'

Vera took a breath in. 'Well Mary, I'd like to know why you are so hungry you have to raid the swill bin?'

Once again Mary hesitated, then said, 'I don't like to tell on my brothers, Miss, because I love 'em, but they eat everything in the house. There's nothing left for me. I get so hungry.' Vera could see her sunken cheeks showed she was undernourished.

'That's not right, is it, constable?' said Mr Parkington who had returned to see how the girls were getting on. 'It's the law that everyone must have their proper food rations.'

'That's quite right, sir. I'll arrest your brothers, Miss Smith.'

'Oh, please, please, don't do that! They don't know I give them everything. They just keep saying they are hungry and is there any more to eat.'

'This is a strange case,' the constable said rubbing his chin as they all looked at the girl's pleading eyes. 'We can't let you starve while your brothers take all your food ration, now can we?'

'And we can't have you living off pig swill either,' said Vera.

Mary muttered, 'They are big men, my brothers, like you gentlemen. They need their meat and gravy, and potatoes and cheese.'

'So do you, Mary.'

'Don't your parents notice you are not getting fed properly?'

'Dad's in the army away somewhere in Africa, I think. Mum's dead. I look after the house and cook as best I can.'

'How old are your brothers?'

'Tom is seventeen. He'll be called up soon and will go into the army like my dad I expect. Mike is fourteen in a few months' time and will be leaving school this summer.'

'And you, Mary, how old are you?'

'I'm sixteen.'

'Very young to be coping on your own,' Vera commented. 'Haven't you any relatives?'

'Not round here. In London. We got bombed out and were moved to Lynn.'

'War casualties should have a lot of help and support.'

The poor girl seemed to be a little less frightened now she was surrounded by people who were not condemning her as much as sympathising with her. So she took a shuddering breath and said, 'Oh, we have been given a house to live in, and they gave us clothes and ration books. But, as I said, the boys love meat so I eat the vegetables they don't like.'

Encouraged, as no-one said anything, Mary explained, 'But sometimes I think I need some other things to eat so I thought, as the British Restaurant throws away left-overs for the pigs, no-one would mind if I came and looked to see if there's anything I could eat. I didn't mean to do anything wrong . . . '

'It's your brothers who are the villains, Mary,' muttered Mr Parkington. 'I'll go and have a word with them.'

'Although you are guilty of breaking the fence, miss,' the constable said taking out his little notebook, 'and I'll have to take you to the police station and charge you for breaking and entering.'

Mary's face crumpled and she began to cry.

It seemed so unfair that this young woman, whose father was fighting for his country, was suffering, when the dance music coming from the hall meant it was full of people enjoying themselves.

'Wait a minute,' said Vera. Everyone looked at her as she put her arm around the girl's bony shoulders. 'Mary needs a good meal first. I'll look in the pantry and see what I can find. In the meantime, I'm sure between us we can solve this problem without making a fuss over a broken fence that can be mended tomorrow.'

'Hear, hear,' said Mr Parkington. 'A couple of stronger nails should soon fix that fence — I dare say I have a hammer and few nails in my car.'

'He keeps everything in that car of his!' Vera commented with a chuckle.

The constable agreed with Mr Parkington to overlook the matter and went on his way.

★ ★ ★

Mary had relished the meal Vera had cooked for her — and Geoff, because he told her he hadn't had any supper. Vera had a cup of tea herself and Geoff said he would accompany Mary home.

Vera sighed as she washed up. She thought about Mary and how her life had been shattered like her home in London. And finding out she was the thief, when she was expecting a completely different outcome. The war certainly produces some surprises. But none better than when she heard Geoff return.

'I thought you'd have gone home,' she said, smiling to see him again as she dried the last plate and put it away.

'I was hoping for the last waltz with you,' he said.

'I'm not dressed for a dance.'

'You look fine to me, Cinderella. Let me take you out of the kitchen for a while.'

Throwing the tea towel in the laundry basket Vera turned to look at his tall figure. He wasn't in uniform, but even in civvies he looked well dressed enough to be a prince. There was nothing spectacular about him really. Good looking, but no pinup.

What she liked about him was . . ., oh, so many things, but she couldn't think of them at the moment in time. But she knew she loved him.

'I'm . . . ' She was going to say she was too tired — because she'd had an exhausting day and she was very tired. Then she remembered she wanted to explain to him, about his letter she didn't receive until too late to say she felt the same way about him as he felt about her — but that was all some time ago now.

She had, unwittingly, refused him. It wasn't her fault. What could she say that would undo the mistake? But she could try. 'As a matter of fact I do like dancing, Geoff. Let's give it a whirl.'

A whirl was not the right word for the excitement she felt coming into the hall and being held by Geoff. His powerful body supported her and she felt faint with the enjoyment of being in his arms. His ability to dance matched her own and she doubted if she'd ever had a better dance partner. But most of all she felt she was enchanted to be dancing the most romantic last dance with him.

She completely forgot that she had to explain to him about his lost letter.

How she resisted kissing him at the end, or him kissing her, when the smooth sounds of the music ceased, she didn't know. It was just clear to her that they both wanted a kiss.

'Well, thank you, Geoff,' she said breathlessly, 'I can't believe you are such a good dancer when you are such an expert at so many other things you do.'

'Ditto,' he said. He seemed to be struggling with his emotions. 'Vera,' he said, 'I can't let you go home alone tonight. And yet . . . I must . . . '

'Listen Geoff,' she said, 'you know I've been meaning to tell you something for ages, but it never seems to be the right time. We must meet and have a talk another time. So please allow me to bike home as I usually do. I'm not afraid of the dark, honestly.'

He seemed reluctant to agree. He took a shuddering breath. 'Yes, I will allow you to go home alone tonight if you promise to go out with me on your day off. Then we'll have plenty of time to sort out what's bothering you.'

She looked up and smiled at his concerned face. 'Of course. I'd love to go out on Friday — if you can make it. I'm off duty.'

'That's great. I think I can manage to wangle a few hours off.'

'You'd better, Geoff Parkington. If

you stand me up — I'll never go out with you again!'

He laughed.

They agreed that a long walk by the river would make a pleasant relaxation on a summer day.

'Are you able to bring some sandwiches, and a flask of tea?' suggested Geoff. 'Then we can wander off and get lost in the countryside.'

'I can do that.'

'And do you mind if I bring the dogs?'

'Of course not. I'd love to see Gip again. It's marvellous that you are able to look after Bill's dog, because I promised Bill that I'd make sure he was taken care of.'

'He has a good life on the farm.'

'I'm sure he does. Bill would be ever so pleased. And so am I, Geoff.'

He said nothing for a few moments. So Vera said, 'Don't think I'm spending all my free time mourning for Bill. He's tucked away in my heart. But I'm pleased to think I could fulfil the last request he made to me, to look after his dog.'

'I do understand.'

Vera believed he did. It was good to talk about mundane things because it gave her a chance to get down to earth again.

She showed him where she had parked her bicycle and he made sure the lights were on before he gave her a quick kiss on the cheek, saying, 'Goodnight, my dear.'

As she wobbled off on her bike she turned round to wave goodbye. And when she got to the end of the road she turned to look back, and there he was, still there watching her go.

When seeing her off on her bicycle Geoff had muttered he had to go and help George and his friends to make sure the hall was in order for the morning. But Vera had the warm feeling that despite that, he was shadowing her in his car all the way home.

A Victory For Vera

It seemed a long time to wait until
Friday. Vera felt jumpy all the working
week and did her best to hide her
strange excitement from the girls. One
hour she seemed to be out of the world
thinking she was likc a fairy happily
floating around everywhere, and the
next she seemed to feel agitated as if
there was something she ought to do
— but couldn't think what it was.

Fortunately the girls were so well
trained she didn't have to worry — only
make sure Gladys was given a hand
now and again, and hadn't forgotten to
do anything.

'I'm being a nuisance to you, aren't
I?' Gladys asked her when Vera came to
assist her with cutting the cabbages as
she was getting behind with her work.

'You, a nuisance, Gladys? Indeed not.
You're a treasure!'

'It's so kind of you to say that. But I know I can't do as much as the others.'

Vera smiled at her anxious face. 'How the country would manage without all the volunteer workers like you I just don't know. You and George are well past retirement age and yet you are both here every day lending a hand. Doing vital work in the kitchen.'

Gladys smiled, but shook her head. 'I keep forgetting things, that's my trouble. I was ever so sorry about that letter I should have given you. Mr Parkington must have wondered why you didn't get it.'

Vera shrugged. 'Don't worry about it.'

Reminded of the letter, Vera decided she would read it again carefully before she saw Geoff. The impression she had, was that he was keen on her. And that because she was engaged, he thought, to Bill, he wasn't going to ask her out.

Well now the situation had changed. Bill no longer had any claim on her. She had had time to get over the shock of his death. And now she felt she shouldn't refuse to love another man — Bill would understand that. Like most young women she wanted to marry and have children. She was looking for someone to replace Bill. And she thought she had found someone — Geoff.

But how shall I tell him that?

But she knew so little about him. She'd even disliked him when she'd first met him. And they had always talked to each other in a most straightforward manner — and she'd been quite rude to him on occasions!

He was older than she was by several years she reckoned. He was a high-ranking officer, and not married as far as she knew. But he seemed a very eligible man. Why hadn't he got a girl? Or, perhaps he had?

On Friday she hoped they would have time to talk and sort things out between them.

★　★　★

The birds awoke Vera on Friday, singing their little hearts out.

It was already light at seven in the morning and, not having to go to work, she had the time to stand at the window and watch several blackbirds who were hopping about looking for worms in the sunny garden she saw after she'd drawn back her bedroom curtains.

It's a beautiful day, Vera Carter. But now the great day has arrived, I do feel nervous. What shall I say to him? How shall I put it that I think I'm in love with him? Am I imagining he is in love with me?

Knowing it was a special day, she looked through her wardrobe and decided a summer dress would be nice to wear — and a cardigan in case it clouded over.

Clothing rations meant her clothing coupons had to be used mainly on replacing underwear, shoes, and warm winter wear. But she had a few pre war summer dresses.

So she selected one, a blue flowered

favourite, thinking Geoff would probably like her to look feminine and not as he usually saw her wrapped up in a kitchen overall.

Her hair could be brushed out too in a film star fashion, not pushed up under a cook's cap.

She hadn't much lipstick left. It was hard to get, but she thought it was right to use some on her lips today.

Twirling around in front of the mirror she decided she really wasn't a bad looking young woman. And it felt great to be prettily dressed for a change.

* * *

'You look nice, dear,' said Mum, when Vera brought her a cup of tea. 'What time is Geoff picking you up?'

'He isn't, he left a message to say where he would meet me.'

'You've got a lovely day for a picnic.'

'Yes we have.' Vera agreed absent-mindedly, thinking there was more at stake at their meeting than having a picnic. But she didn't mention that to her mother.

'I'd like to take a few of those little tomatoes you're growing in the greenhouse just now, Mum. Do you mind?'

'Of course you can — if we can find any ripe enough. I'm only too pleased to think a nice man like Geoff will enjoy them.'

'May I use your shopping basket for our picnic things?'

'Go ahead.'

'Mum, as it's such a sunny day, may I borrow your sun hat?'

'You may,' said Mum, taking a sip of her tea. 'It's up on top of my wardrobe in the round hat box. It should go very nicely with your dress.'

Vera clambered on a chair to reach the box, and opening it she reached to take out a wide brimmed straw hat. It was light and had a wide band decorated with clusters of pink and pale blue artificial flowers, and had long silky ribbons hanging down the back.

She put it on and asked, 'Do you

think he'll like me in this, Mum?'

'Well he seemed to like you enough in a cook's cap, so I expect he'll like you in that.'

Vera grinned.

She was just about to leave the bedroom when she stopped and poked her head around the door. 'And can you spare a bottle of beer for Geoff? I know you normally keep a couple for special occasions, but a man likes a drink — especially on a hot day.'

'I'd have thought you'd go to a pub for a drink.'

'Maybe we will. Only Geoff said he is keen for us to lose ourselves in the countryside.'

Mum shook her finger at her. 'Don't you allow him to take you away too far, dear.'

Vera giggled as she ran downstairs.

★   ★   ★

Vera had got off the bus with the picnic basket and stood at the crossroads with nothing to see but fields, trees and hedges — and some curious cows, who came to look at her while chewing the cud as they flicked their tails lazily.

She waited. And waited. Am I at the right place?

She looked at her watch for the sixth time since she'd got there, wondering if she had got the time or the place of the meeting wrong.

Mr Parkington, where are you? Half an hour had gone by since she'd got off the bus and the only sounds she heard were of buzzing bees, a tractor in the distance, and some birds giving her a merry tune.

As it was warm and sunny, she sat down at the side of the road and dozed amongst the long grasses and wild flowers, with her hat shading her face. After another quarter of an hour, she looked at the picnic basket and felt cross. And wondered if she should eat the contents up, cross over the road and catch the bus back home.

She must have slept and was awoken

by a lick on the nose. A furry face looked down at her. She blinked in the sunshine as, sitting up, she saw two dogs jumping about in front of her, and barking.

'Ah, there you are!' She recognised Geoff's mellow voice. 'Sorry we're so late.'

Yes, it was him all right walking casually towards her. Dressed in a short-sleeved open-necked shirt, and white slacks, showing he intended to go out for a walk in the countryside.

She wasn't sure if she was delighted to see him — or mad with him for being so late. But the nap had refreshed her and she rose up on her feet to see both dogs had their noses in her picnic basket.

Geoff shooed them away, and taking a knapsack from his shoulders he said, 'Shall I put this stuff into my bag? It will save carrying the basket?'

As he was doing it anyway, Vera said nothing.

'There we are, that's done,' he said,

doing up the straps of his canvas bag and easing it on his wide shoulders.

'What about Mum's shopping basket? I can't leave it here.'

'I'll put it in my car.'

'I didn't hear you drive up.'

'You were asleep. A very sensible thing to do. I'd expect a girl like you to think of something useful to do with your time while you waited for me. You're not the type to stand there fuming because I kept you waiting.'

What could she say?

'Now, let me see which way we should go.' He was looking at the crossroads. 'Since the war they have removed all the signposts around here to say where the roads lead to, in case there is an invasion. But I've brought an army map and compass with me.'

He opened up the map and looked intently at it. 'Here we are. And over there is the ancient pedlar track. I think it's the best way to go.' He pointed ahead. 'Do you agree?'

She nodded; how would she know?

But it was surprisingly comforting to be feeling somehow protected now that he was here. He gave her a sense of security.

He allowed her to feel she was being looked after — like he looked after his dogs.

'Battle. Gip. Heel.'

Amazingly the dogs obeyed him. But then wasn't she being obedient as she trotted along with him?

He turned to beam at her. 'You look enchanting in your dress, and hat, Vera. Good enough to eat.'

'I hope you'll be satisfied with the sandwiches.'

He laughed and put his arm around her and gave her a kiss. 'Sorry I was late. It seems there was an air raid last night and the dogs heard the low flying aircraft and air raid siren and scampered off in fright. I had to search for Gip. He'd run for miles.'

'Oh dear. Was there a raid? Did anywhere get bombed?'

'A couple of houses in Peterborough

I was told. A German fighter dumping his bombs before going home they reckon. It wasn't targeted on anything we think.'

Vera shivered as she looked up at the blue sky. No-one was safe in wartime. You just didn't normally think about it and got on with your job.

Still dumbstruck by the way he'd turned up and organised things so quickly, she watched as he strode off with Mum's basket, and locked it in his car he'd tucked behind an open gate off the road.

*   *   *

It was a good choice for a walk. Norfolk countryside at its best. But Vera's thoughts were only partly on what she was seeing.

Wondering what to say, despite the many times she had gone over it in her mind, she was pleased when Geoff began to talk.

'Vera,' he said, 'I was wondering if

you could bring yourself to reconsider our relationship now? I know it's not long after Bill's death, and you will always feel no-one can replace him . . . but perhaps you are ready to find someone else?'

Knowing how difficult she found it to talk about the same matter, she said, 'Geoff, you have said what I feel exactly.'

He took her hand and squeezed it. 'So now I have a chance of winning your affection?'

'Yes,' she smiled up at him.

They walked together. No more words were necessary for a while. Then he said, 'I expect you want to know more about me.'

She looked up into his eyes. 'Of course I do.'

He explained how his parents owned hotels and that after the war he thought he might go into the hotel business.

He talked as though he knew the war would end eventually. And as a senior army officer he should have a better idea about that than most people.

'Do you still think we are going to win the war?'

'I think we will, in time. However, there are many hard battles yet to be won, but the tide is turning against our enemies. We've just got to struggle on. Be steadfast, like you are, Vera.'

She loved holding his hand. 'I think I shall be able to be stronger with you.'

'That applies to me too. I need your support, Vera. I've already gained from knowing you, and being able to share my troubles.'

'Troubles shared are troubles halved — so they say.'

They laughed.

'Tell me about your family, Geoff.'

He told her he had two brothers, one married, and one a prisoner-of-war captured at Dunkirk.

'That's dreadful for your family.'

'It is. But the Red Cross send us his letters, which is some comfort for my parents to know he is surviving. But as the war will go on for some time he'll need some settling when he gets back home.' He thought for a moment and added, 'We'll all need to adjust after the war.'

'Yes,' agreed Vera, so would she, but she understood he was thinking of his own heavy responsibility, and the many men who were in danger of losing their lives before the conflict ended.

They stopped and enjoyed their picnic, and so did the dogs, as Geoff had brought some dog biscuits for them.

Their pleasant summer walk ended as they returned footsore to his car.

They stopped on the way home and got some fish and chips.

'This is first class nourishment,' said Vera. 'Three pence for the fish, and two pence for the chips. It's British food at its best.'

'You should know all about that. I just enjoy my fish and chips.'

She rested her head contentedly against his shoulder. And then they turned to look into each other's eyes, and kissed.

No more needed to be said.

The dogs were asleep in the back of the car, snoring gently, after gobbling up the scraps of the fish and chips.

Vera wanted those wonderful minutes with him to last forever.

* * *

Next morning, the previous day seemed like a dream as Vera got ready for work. A precious dream. She resented having to go back to work — or even having to answer her mother's questions about her day out.

It was all so private she didn't want to discuss the wonderful feeling she had about it all with anyone. Fortunately no-one knew she'd been out with Mr Parkington, so no-one questioned her. She was able to go about her usual jobs without thinking so much about what she had to do.

Her mind was returning constantly to Geoff, and thinking what a wonderful man she was lucky enough to have found.

The girls at work were singing that

day, and it was a cheerful place with much laughter as they worked hard to get a meal ready for midday.

They were about to serve up when Vera suddenly came down to earth.

Where were the sausages she'd put in the oven half-an-hour ago?

Then the awful truth dawned on her.

She hadn't put them in.

Embarrassed, she had to admit her mistake to her fellow cooks.

'I'm sorry,' she said, red-faced before them.

How they all laughed. Sally was shrieking with laughter and Margaret couldn't stop, while Gladys wiped the tears from her eyes.

The uproar greeted Mr Parkington as he came into the kitchen to know why the meal wasn't ready.

Everyone was laughing so much he couldn't get any sense out of them for a few minutes.

'We have a hundred people in the hall waiting for their meal. Where is it?' He sounded cross.

Vera spoke up at last. 'Mr Parkington. I'm sorry to say I thought I had put the sausages in the oven — but I didn't.'

'She forgot to put them in, sir,' giggled Sally.

He seemed quite shocked.

'Right,' he boomed as if he was a sergeant on the parade ground, 'Miss Carter, that is sheer negligence. I'm giving you the sack!'

The kitchen became silent. The laughter died out immediately and faces became horror struck.

'I'm sure it's my fault really, Mr Parkington,' said Gladys coming forward and looking up anxiously at the stern-looking man. 'I expect I was told to put the oven on and I forgot. I'm always forgetting things.'

Vera could spot the twinkle in his eyes, and recovering, took a deep breath and said, 'No, Gladys, it's not your fault. It's entirely mine. Now we'll have to open some tins of Spam right away. So serve up the soup, and that will give the diners something to start with.'

As the ladies rushed to get the soup pan out into the hall, Mr Parkington announced that he would come and speak to them all later. Then he returned into the hall for his meal grumbling that he would try and calm the waiting customers, and like most people he preferred sausages to Spam, and that was a shame Vera had been so careless.

But swinging round he gave Vera a private wink before he left the kitchen.

'He can't sack you! Can he?' Sally asked fearfully.

'He just did.'

'But you've only made one mistake, Miss. Like we all do at times.'

Gladys came up to her with a worried face, saying, 'It's me he should get rid of — not you. You tell him how many times I have let you down by forgetting this and that.'

Margaret looked outraged. 'I'll have a word with him, Vera. Don't you worry. Mr Parkington just doesn't appreciate what a fine cook and organiser you are. I'll tell him we'll all go to pieces if he gets rid of you. Over such a trivial matter too! As you say we can serve up Spam in a jiffy. Give me the key to the store cupboard and I'll get some tins out and slice up the meat.'

Vera blessed them all for being so supportive and bustling around to overcome the hitch she'd created. But she wished Mr Parkington hadn't been quite so severe in the way he'd talked to them.

But he had promptly restored a busy working atmosphere in the kitchen. Which made the dinner ladies buckle to and produce the usual high standard of food for the waiting diners.

The pace quietened down as the meal came to an end. As the plates were wheeled out to be washed, Vera felt pleased that her chocolate sponge pudding turned out to be a great success with the customers, and they forgot to complain that they hadn't had what was written on the menu, and hadn't been given sausages for the main course.

'Whew! I'm glad that's over!' remarked Margaret taking a pile of dirty plates over to the sink where Gladys and Sally were busy washing up.

'It isn't yet,' remarked Gladys, up to her elbows in soapy water.

'What do you mean?' said Margaret. 'I've cleared all the tables and wiped them down. I'm sure there aren't any more dirty dishes about, Gladys.'

'What about the dirty looks, Margaret? He looked daggers at Vera. Says he's going to sack her, remember?'

Margaret gave a sigh as she wiped her brow with the back of her hand. 'Don't you worry about what he says. I've known Geoffrey Parkington since he was a boy — '

'You didn't tell us that!'

'No, well, it's a long story. Anyway, I know he's a bit of a dark horse. He is very bright — and very kind. I should know because he helped me when I was in difficulties. But I never said anything because he asked me not to.'

'Well I never!'

'He was probably only keen to get us all moving quickly to get the meal served or there'd have been a riot out there in the hall if all those people had paid their nine pence, and there was nothing to eat.'

Gladys was not convinced and muttered to herself as she finished the washing up.

Sally collected and rinsed out the tea towels then hung them up on the clothes line, but she was not singing, *My bonny lies over the ocean*, as she usually did.

As Vera came past by her Sally said, 'Cor, Mr Parkington's in a right mood today, Miss. Do you think he meant it when he says you have to go?'

'When you've finished hanging up the tea towels, will you make the tea please, Sally?'

'Do you think it will soften him up?'

Vera ignored her speculation and chivvied all the assistants into tidying up the kitchen especially well as she reminded them Mr Parkington said he was coming to talk to them.

* * *

Later, as they sat around the table looking gloomily at each other, they heard Mr Parkington's footsteps and were surprised when he ushered a thin, shy girl into the kitchen.

'I want you to meet Mary Smith, everyone. She's coming to work here.'

As the ladies looked at the timid girl, Vera got up and, putting her arm around Mary, said, 'That's great news. I'm sure you'll be happy working here.'

'Instead of Vera?' blurted out Sally.

Mr Parkington replied, 'Yes, Miss Williams.'

Margaret protested, 'If Vera had more help she wouldn't have made that mistake.'

He cleared his throat. 'Not so, Miss Smallwood. I'm well aware that mistakes are rarely made in this kitchen. You all work well together. But the person in charge has to be very responsible. And that is why you will be taking Vera's place. You're quite capable of doing her job.'

Margaret looked flabbergasted.

Gladys had tears in her eyes as she rubbed her hands together. 'Mr Parkington,' she said in a quavering voice, 'I think . . . it should be me who should go.'

'Do you want to, Mrs Munchie?'

'No, no, Mr Parkington. But . . . '

He finished her sentence. 'I believe you could do with an easier working day. Am I right to suggest you would be happier doing less hours? Perhaps come in to help prepare the vegetables daily? And help young Mary here to learn to do some of your work?'

Mary nodded enthusiastically. 'I'd like to help you, Mrs Munchie.'

Gladys looked confused.

'Yes,' Vera replied for her, thinking she would explain to Gladys later that her shorter working day helping in the kitchen would still be appreciated, and that as an older lady she needed to take things more easily than the younger, fitter women.

'You shouldn't be taking Vera from us!' shouted Sally belligerently, banging her tea enamel mug on the table.

Mr Parkington held up his hands as if in surrender, and smiled.

'Now I must explain about Vera — and me.'

Everyone's surprised eyes looked at him. Not a sound was heard in the normally noisy kitchen.

He moved behind to where Vera was sitting and put his hands on her shoulders. 'I confess I feel a cad taking Vera from you. But I need her.'

'For what?' yelled Sally.

'Vera has done me the honour of agreeing to be my wife.'

After a stunned silence, shouts of joy erupted.

'Congratulations!'

'Well I'll be . . . '

'Crikey, Mr Parkington! You've been having us on!'

Vera sat blushing and smiled widely. She couldn't think of anything to say. One thing she couldn't say, was to deny it.

Margaret saved the situation by saying, 'Geoff Parkington, you are a lucky man. And Vera, you are a lucky lady.'

'Hear, hear!' The hearty cheers were so loud anyone outside might think the war had been won.

George popped in from the hall to see what all the commotion was about, and resting his hands on his sweeping brush looked amazed at first, and then chuckled to see Mr Parkington kissing Vera.

As for Vera, winning Geoff, the man she loved, was indeed a victory.

THE END

We do hope that you have enjoyed reading this large print book.

Did you know that all of our titles are available for purchase?

We publish a wide range of high quality large print books including:
Romances, Mysteries, Classics
General Fiction
Non Fiction and Westerns

Special interest titles available in large print are:
The Little Oxford Dictionary
Music Book, Song Book
Hymn Book, Service Book

Also available from us courtesy of Oxford University Press:
Young Readers' Dictionary
(large print edition)
Young Readers' Thesaurus
(large print edition)

For further information or a free brochure, please contact us at:
Ulverscroft Large Print Books Ltd.,
The Green, Bradgate Road, Anstey,
Leicester, LE7 7FU, England.
Tel: (00 44) **0116 236 4325**
Fax: (00 44) **0116 234 0205**

FALLING LEAVES

Sheila Benton

When Richard employs Annie to update the computer system for his company, she finds herself, through circumstance, living in his house. Although they are attracted to each other, Richard's daughter, Katie, takes a dislike to her. Added to this, Annie suspects that Richard is in love with someone else, so she allows herself to be drawn to Steve, Richard's accountant. Annie feels she must choose between love and a career — how can the complications in her life be resolved . . . ?

ENCHANTED VOYAGE

Mavis Thomas

Lauren was a reluctant member of the family holiday group on a sea cruise, taking in Italy, Greece and Turkey. All her thoughts were of him: she agonised over Grant's accident, his operation, and his forthcoming marriage — to Elaine . . . However, whilst on the *Bella Italia*, Lauren became deeply involved with a charismatic member of the entertainment team . . . and a fellow passenger — a teacher and his two difficult children . . .

WHERE THE BLUEBELLS GROW WILD

Wendy Kremer

Stephen employs Sara, a landscape designer, to improve the appearance of the gardens of Knowles House, his Georgian mansion. He wants to use innovative ideas to generate additional sources of income and is hoping to hire it out for special events — an attractive garden would boost his chances. Lucy, Stephen's childhood friend, lives with her father on the adjoining country estate. Everyone thinks Lucy and Stephen are made for each other — but then along comes Sara . . .

THE BUTTERFLY DANCE

Rosemary A. Smith

It's 1902 and life, for Katherine Johnson, has been rather mundane, living with her Aunt Phoebe and Uncle Zachariah in their house on the coast. However, on her twentieth birthday, she meets Kane O'Brien on the beach and suddenly her thoughts are all of him. But will the circumstances of Kane's birth prevent her Aunt from accepting their love for one another? What is the mystery of the beautiful keepsake box? And where will the butterfly dance lead them?

LONG SHADOWS

Margaret Mounsdon

When Fiona Dalrymple's grand-mother dies, Fiona is shocked to learn that Doreen wasn't actually her grandmother at all . . . Her grand-father's first wife, Ellie Marsden, is still alive and when Fiona meets her, Ellie has a further shock for Fiona: she also has a brother. What's more, Tim has disappeared and Fiona is charged with the task of finding him . . . so why does Rory, Tim's handsome boss, seems intent on being more of a hindrance than a help?